I0718055

BLENDED *hearts*

Katrina Marie

Wee One, this is for you. Raising you during your teen years has been a rollercoaster. But I'm so incredibly proud of you. Thank you for the inspiration for Alexandra.

prologue

. . .

A RETIREMENT ANNOUNCEMENT? Tonight?

Dad implied it would be years before he left Starlit Fields to us kids. Now it's happening sooner than any of us imagined. Well, except Pierce, he seems to be in the know about everything. A few of my other siblings as well.

The only ones shocked by the announcement are me, Piper, and Paula. I'm usually the one Pierce confides in. The person he's always been able to rely on. What makes this night different than any other?

I watch my baby sister, Piper, storm off the porch. She's never been able to hide her emotions. I used to tease her about it when we were kids. Showing how you feel always seemed like a weakness.

Right now, though, I'd give anything to be able to show the frustration flowing through every inch of me. She would laugh if she knew how jealous I am of her confidence in herself.

Glasses clinking and congratulations pepper the air

around me and for once, I don't want to partake. Piper has the right idea. I follow the path she took because there is only once place, she could be going.

I take my time walking toward our childhood swing set. I don't want Piper to think I'm hovering. It's the one thing she has complained about since we were kids. Apparently, the big siblings hover too much.

"I thought I might find you over here." Piper is sitting in one of the swings and jumps at the sound of my voice.

"Peter? Why aren't you eating with everyone else?" She sounds sad. Not that I can blame her. The news took at least half of us by surprise.

"I didn't much feel like it." I press down on the swing next to her, making sure it can hold my weight, and take a seat.

"So, you really didn't know Dad was announcing his retirement tonight? I figured being so close to Pierce would make you privy to this sort of information."

It takes me a few moments to answer her. Because she's not wrong. Up until tonight, I thought I knew everything Pierce did.

"Yeah, I thought so, too." I shuffle my feet in the dirt, making two tracks.

"It sucks being on this side of information, doesn't it?"

I flinch at the words. I know she doesn't mean anything by them. At least, not completely. I know a dig when I hear it. The feeling isn't any better, though. Being on this side of finding out, isn't fun. If anything, it puts how the rest of my siblings feel into perspective.

"Yep." I nod and swing slightly. The fear of going too high and falling off keeps me from letting go completely.

"Maybe I've been putting too much of myself into the winery and being at Pierce's beck and call."

"I could have told you that." She snorts and swings a bit higher. "You've been so far up his ass since we were kids I didn't know where he ended and you began."

I gag at the insult. That's really how the rest of them see me. As a kiss ass ready to do whatever Pierce wants. It's not exactly hard to deny since I constantly do everything. But he always makes it sound like nobody else will take care of things. I need to have more faith in my brothers and sisters.

"That is not a great visual. You could have put that more eloquently."

"Not really." She shakes her head. "It's literally the only way to describe your relationship to our elder brother. Take a step back, you might realize you're a completely different person."

The sigh passing through my lips is louder than I thought. Hopefully she doesn't hear it. How pathetic is it that I'm getting lectured by my baby sister? She's never been afraid to go after what she wants, even when Pierce consistently shoots her down. She gets up and tries again.

I don't even know who I am without the winery. So many years have been spent proving to Pierce that I'm capable of doing everything he does. That he can count on me. His opinion of me has been the only thing pushing me forward. Even as far back as my teen years.

Do I even have any hobbies? The only thing I do outside of work is hang out with Miles at the bar. Sometimes we'll go to the next town over and play pool. Shit, I'm turning into my big brother. That's just…sad. Nobody wants to wake up one day realizing all they do is work.

Piper drags her feet on the ground, slowing down the momentum of the swing. An owl hoots in the distance, and I didn't realize how dark it's gotten. I didn't think we'd been away from the back porch that long. Time flies when you have the sudden realization you have no idea who you are as a person. I'm pretty sure I'm too young for a mid-life crisis, but maybe not.

"Do you think we should get back?" I nudge Piper's shoulder as soon as she comes to a stop. "I'm sure they'll send out a search party for us."

"You can head back." She nods her head toward the house. "I'll be up in a minute. Just need to fix my expression and gather my wits."

"Okay, don't be too long or I'll be back to drag you to the house. You need to eat something."

I had the good sense to eat a snack before we got started. Piper probably didn't. She has a habit of forgetting to take care of herself when she's caught up in something.

"You act like I haven't been stealing bites the whole time we've been here."

I shake my head as I stand. "Why am I not surprised? Somehow, you're the only one who gets away with it. At least, without getting your hand smacked."

"Gotta have quick reflexes, big brother."

She waves her hands toward me showing me just how fast she is. She's not, but she doesn't realize she could get away with murder because she's the baby. Not that we made life easy for her growing up. She was the smallest and knew how to press our buttons.

I don't think she realizes how much she got on our nerves back then. Not that she would care. She takes up space no matter where she goes and I admire her for that.

"You are such a dork." I turn back toward the path from the house. "You've got, ten minutes. If you aren't at the house, I'll send reinforcements."

"Yeah, yeah."

I steal a quick glance over my shoulder to see if she's going to move, but she's literally waving me away. That is not what I expected. I'm not sure why, though. I guess I thought she'd stand and follow after me like she did when we were kids. A part of me misses it, even though it was annoying back then.

She always wanted to hang out with her big brothers and sister. Now…she does everything she can to avoid us, except for Parker and Paula. Piper is right, though. I need to live my life and not devote all of it to Starlit Fields. The only problem is, I don't know how.

one

. . .

peter

IF ONE MORE PERSON COMES IN this building I'm going to lose it. Every year it's the same thing. People all of a sudden realize it's New Year's Eve and rush to grab the alcohol they forgot to purchase for their parties.

The fact they're making bottles of wine fall off the shelf isn't the problem. It's the part where they wait until the last possible second to come in. Now would be a perfect time for Pierce to look at being stocked in stores. We can do other things to bring people to the winery. I know Piper has some ideas. She was telling me about them in the Fall.

"Peter, we need three more bottles of sangria." Phillip hollers from the backyard of the main building. He's lucky I have the door open and can hear him.

"I'm coming with a whole case. Give me a few seconds."

"Speed it up."

Pfft. He thinks rushing me is going to make me move

faster, he has another thing coming. I'm ready for the day to be over so I can go home and play video games.

"We should have closed early today." I grumble as I load a case with bottles of sangria. Piper needs to stop telling our followers it's her favorite. We can barely keep it in stock.

Lifting the case I head toward the door. I probably should have grabbed a dolly to take in more. But…the less time I spend in the main building the less I have to interact with people.

There is a line to the door when I walk into the main house. Am I surprised? No. Not in the slightest. The only plus side to us being this busy today is the rest of the day will go by quickly. I can't rest when I'm running crates back and forth.

"Peter, can you jump back here and help me get this line moving?" Piper asks as she takes a credit card from a customer.

Of course she'd ask. Where are literally any of our other siblings? It's funny how all of them have disappeared when we have a full house.

"Do you really need me? I was going to grab a few more crates to get us through the day."

Instead of answering, she glares at me. Point taken. You'd think she'd be nicer to me since I was the one who took care of her when she was upset with Beau and our eldest brother a few months ago. But, I know if she's asking for help, she really needs it.

I set the crate of wine against the wall and rush over to the other kiosk. Piper knows I'll do anything to help her out after we've bonded over the past few months.

She's been trying, unsuccessfully, to get me to take

time off work and have fun. She even has Miles on board. Not that he's complaining too much. It means more time playing pool and watching him try to hit on women. While funny, it's not how I want to spend my time.

"Which of our fine wines can I get for you today?" I ask the customer who moved lines. She stares at the list of wines taped to the counter.

"Let me look over the list really quick." She says without meeting my eyes.

The only thing they don't seem to understand is I love working. It's the one task I'm good at. Besides working helps me forget I have no life. Even if it means working with Pierce.

I still haven't forgiven him for keeping Dad's early retirement a secret. Or, the fact him and Beau were pretty much lying to Piper. She's working toward mending that hurt with our brother after already making up with her boyfriend. Me? It's not that easy.

Geez, could this woman make her selection any slower? No wonder the line is so long. People have no clue what they want. Or, maybe they don't know what we offer.

I glance over at Piper while I'm waiting. She points to her mouth and lifts it up in a smile. What the hell is she trying to tell me?

She points at me before pointing back to her face. Oh, she wants me to smile. Okay, got it. I give her a thumbs up before turning back to the customer still looking over the wine selections.

"Is there a certain type you generally like? Sweet? Or dry?" Honestly, at this point I'm trying to get her to buy her bottles and go. There are still way too many people waiting in line.

"I'm partial to sweet wines." She runs her finger down the list of sweet wines. "Do you have a favorite?"

A part of me wishes this customer would have stayed in Piper's line. "I like most of them. But if you like sweet, sangria is always a good choice. We also have one with cranberry that's similar to that. My sister's favorite is sangria, though." I nod my head in her direction so she can put a face with the recommendation.

"That settles it." The woman looks up and grins. "I'll take two bottles of sangria, and a bottle of the cranberry one you were talking about."

"Absolutely, let me grab those bottles for you." I grab two bottles from the grate I brought in moments ago, and pull our cranberry off the shelf.

The bags are on the shelf under the kiosks and I pull the medium sized one out. I gently place the bottles inside and take the woman's payment.

"Thank you, I hope these are as good as you say they are." She pulls the bag off the counter and turns toward the exit.

Of course they are, I wouldn't have suggested them otherwise. That would be rude to say out loud. "Happy New Year."

It's the one thing I can say right now that won't be horrible. And, I can say it with a straight face.

Piper and I work in silence, only talking to the customers, until the line is finally at a manageable length.

"Are you going to the party at Ashes tonight?" Piper asks as she rings up another person and hands them their bag of wine.

"I don't know yet." I shrug and move to toward the now empty crate. "Parties like that aren't really my thing."

"Come on," Piper sighs. "Come out and live a little. It's not like you've taken my advice to make more time for yourself. Tonight is the perfect chance to do it." She turns toward me now that we have an empty room. "That should be your New Year's resolution. Stop working so damn much and learn how to have a good time."

"I'm perfectly capable of having a good time at home."

"Drinking while playing video games by yourself is not a good time."

Well, that's a bit judgmental. I happen to have a blast hanging out at home. "I don't even have anyone to go with."

"Neither does Parker, but he's still going."

As if that is a sound argument to use with me. Parker will do pretty much anything. He craves being around people. It boosts his ego higher than normal.

Piper takes a step toward me, giving me puppy dog eyes. It's how she got her way when we were kids, and I'll be damned if it works now.

"Please, Peter. What if I said it was my New Year's wish to have my big brothers with me to celebrate?"

"Does that extend to Phillip and Pierce?" I'm curious what her answer is.

"Um, sure. I mean if they want to go. I think Phillip is going already. If Pierce goes, he'll only bring down the mood."

I let my baby sister squirm for a moment. It's not like I'll have to pay to get in. Paula and Tristan got all of us passes. It's one of the perks of dating someone who works with Crooked Halo I guess.

"Fine, I'll go." I hold my hands up as she jumps to hug me. "But I'm not dressing up. You'll be lucky if I stay until midnight."

She releases me and scoffs. "You have to."

My only answer is a shrug as I pick up the crate and leave the main house. Of course, I'll stay until midnight, but I'll let her worry over it for the rest of the night.

There are too many people in this bar. This is the one reason I didn't want to come out tonight. Yes, I know most of the people here on some level. I'm sure we've crossed paths at some point, but that doesn't necessarily mean I want to spend my night off with them.

Crooked Halo is on stage playing songs I haven't heard before. It must be the music they were working on a few months ago. It's peeled back and nothing like they've released before. So far, this is the only upside to my evening. We get to hear the new music before the masses. It's special.

"Would you stop looking so glum?" Piper bumps into my arm. "It's a night meant for new beginnings."

"I'm merely enjoying the music. If you don't like my vibe, go bug Parker."

"Nah," she shakes her head.

Beau raises his voice. "I think he's trying to hit on someone right now."

"Of course he is," I mumble. He's always trying to get some sort of date and doesn't give up. One of these days that arrogance is going to bite him in the ass.

"We only have a few more minutes until midnight." Piper squeals.

Her excitement makes me smile. The way she can always have a positive outlook is inspiring. If only I could have that sunny disposition after getting screwed over. She's a forgive and mostly forget type of person. I…hold grudges.

Should I? Absolutely not. I can't help it though. At least, not when it comes to Pierce. Not when he treated me like an equal then didn't keep me in the loop. The sad thing is he doesn't even feel bad about it. He didn't offer any kind of apology to any of us. Except for Piper. But he was already in the dog house with her. I don't blame her one bit.

Which is another thing he kept under wraps. I don't understand why it was so important for him to not let anyone in on the fact he knew about Piper doing the marketing the way she wanted. It was a shitty thing to do to her.

"Ten, nine, eight." The shout of everyone counting down until the new year breaks me from my thoughts.

Maybe I do need to be more like Piper. This year I'm going in with a focus on me.

"Five. Four. Three. Two. One. HAPPY NEW YEAR." Everyone screams and I join in with them. Things are changing and I might as well change with them.

Both Piper and Beau pull me into a group hug to bring in the new year. They didn't leave me out, and I'm grateful. The rest of the crowd is too busy making out with their dates.

"I think I'm going to head out." This is not my scene and I can hear my sofa calling my name. Maybe Miles will be up for some video games. Assuming he isn't out and about. If he was here, I'd at least have someone to talk to. Actually, scratch that. He'd be just like Parker trying to find a date for the night.

It's been a few weeks since I've seen him. Or heard from him for that matter. We need to fix that. Mostly because I need space from my family.

"No, don't leave." Piper's voice is high pitched. "Stay a little longer."

"Sorry, sis." I wrap my arm around her for a quick hug. "I'm wiped after moving crates of sangria all day."

It's not a complete lie. Between that and standing in the bar because there aren't any empty tables, my feet are killing me.

"Fine." She pouts. "I'll come by tomorrow. We need to make sure you take your resolution to heart."

Ignoring her statement, I wave at Beau before turning toward the door. At least I parked across the street. The fight against traffic won't be an issue.

Within twenty minutes I'm driving down Starlit Road. Music is my companion as I make my way down the dark road to my driveway.

A blur of motion catches my eye and I slow down. What the hell was that? It's too big to be a possum, but too small to be livestock.

I slow the truck's motion to a crawl, trying to find whatever it is in my headlights. There isn't anything, but then I spy a glint of metal further up the road. Instead of driving closer to whatever it is, I open my door and grab the flashlight from my console. Getting hit in the new year is not on my list of goals.

My steps are slow and measured as I make my way

toward the animal. The closer I get, I can see it's a dog. Damn, I should have brought something it could eat. If only to coax it toward me.

Right as my hand slips around the dog's collar, a loud boom echoes across the countryside and sparkles light up the sky. The dog jumps and tries to bolt. Apparently, this pup is scared of fireworks. I pull it close to me and try to see if there's a tag on the collar.

Alice is stamped into the metal tag adorning her collar. The only other information is a phone number and a town in Oklahoma.

"You're a long way from home," I whisper to pup. "Let's get you somewhere safe while I try to find your owner, Alice."

She licks my hand and I take it as a sign of trust. I'm only glad I found her before she really got lost...or worse.

two

. . .

callie

"MOM, WE HAVE TO FIND HER." Alexandra's voice is high pitched and panicked. I don't blame her. Alice is her dog. The two of them connected immediately when we found her at the shelter.

"We will." I reassure her. "We're just waiting on Uncle Miles to get here. We don't have a vehicle that can go off-road. Who knows where Alice could have run off to."

It's not an exaggeration either. There are miles of fields behind surrounding our new house. Talk about a way to bring in the new year. Single and now with a missing dog.

"It's all my fault." Alexandra buries her face in her hands. "I thought they were done popping fireworks. She needed to go potty. I didn't think the silence was only an intermission."

"It's okay sweetie. We'll find her." Or maybe someone else has and I should be watching my phone. "I should have warned you about how it can be in the country when it's time for fireworks. It's one of the few places you can set them off without getting a ticket."

"Well, that sounds like a them problem," She huffs.

I pull my teenager into my arms and rock her back and forth. It worked when she was a baby, and I'm hoping it has the same effect at soothing her now. At least until my brother gets here to search for our dog.

I don't remember the last time I was on this road prior to buying this house, and I'd have no idea where to look. Hurry up, Miles.

There's a knock at the door, and Alexandra jumps out of my arms to answer it. You'd think at fourteen she knows the whole stranger danger thing, but apparently, I'm going to have reiterate the lesson. Especially since we're in a newish area. Well, new to her, not me. I grew up here.

"Uncle Miles…finally!" Alexandra is still panicked. Her voice is loud and shrill. It hurts even my ears and I'm in another room.

"What do you mean 'finally'? I live on the other side of town. With all the parties happening tonight, it took me a bit to get here." His arm is around Alexandra's shoulder, comforting her as best he can, as he walks into the living room. "How long has Alice been gone?"

"A few hours?" I'm not really sure. We searched all around our property and part of the way down the road. "We didn't want to be on the road in the dark with the possibility of getting hit by some drunk driver."

"That's smart. I will drive the back area of the property along the trees. If we're lucky, she'll come back home on her own."

"But how will she know this is home?" Alexandra sniffles. "We just moved here. The only scent she truly knows is our house back in Oklahoma."

"Then we'll have to hope someone finds her." Miles glances over at me. "Did she have on a collar with your number?"

All I can do is nod. It kills me to see my daughter this heartbroken. But I know exactly how she feels. We've had Alice since she was a puppy…she's family.

"Can I go with you to search the tree line?" Alexandra leans into her uncle. "I don't think I can sit here and do nothing much longer. Maybe if I'm with you, she'll hear my voice and come to me."

"That's a good idea." Miles smiles down at her. "While we're out looking, I need you to do something, Callie."

"Whatever you need." I'm also feeling pretty useless.

"Get some of your clothes and Alexandras and place them around the yard. It'll help Alice find your scent."

"I can do that." I grab my phone off the coffee table and wave it in the air. "If she comes back, I'll give you a call."

I watch my brother and daughter rush out of the house. As much as I didn't want to move back home, in this very moment, I'm glad. There's no way I would have known the thing about the clothes. I mean, I guess I could have searched online for things to do, but I don't think I would have had the inkling to do it.

Crap. I don't know what kind of clothes and I don't really want to put any of the clean ones out there. I just finished getting almost everything washed. Clothes being in boxes smell stale and I couldn't handle it.

I dial my brother's number.

"Is she back?" Not even a hello. Not that I blame him.

"No, but I have a question. Do the clothes need to be clean?"

"Dirty clothes work best. Your scent is fresher."

"Thanks. Good luck." I don't even bother waiting for him to reply. I'm sure Alexandra is driving him bananas.

At least I haven't gotten around to washing the clothes in our suitcase. We took a couple of detours on our way down here. Completely unnecessary, but I needed to do something to ease Alexandra into the move. She wasn't happy about leaving her friends behind. She didn't seem to mind not seeing her dad on a regular basis. Not that she did anyway. He found any excuse he could to shirk his responsibilities.

Shoving my phone in my pocket, I rush to Alexandra's room and dig through the pile of clothes on her floor. I'm not sure how far away from the house I need to place the clothes, so I grab an armful.

Next stop is my room. My dirty clothes are in a basket at the foot of my bed, and I drop Alexandra's on top. I rummage through the boxes against the wall for a flashlight. I may have grown up in the country but I don't want to encounter any of the wildlife.

With the flashlight and basket in hand, I head toward the front door. I'll start at the front of the house and work my way around. I open the door, but don't bother closing it. What if Alice comes back while I'm in the back? I don't want her getting scared again and running in the opposite direction.

Miles didn't say how far out to put the laundry. I set one piece down close to the house, walk out about five feet and set another one. Then another few feet and set down a third piece. I want Alice to have multiple pieces of our scent. Anything to make it easier for her to find her way home.

I continue this pattern all the way around the house. There's no way in hell I'm going to leave a section unguarded. If Alice doesn't come back, my daughter will be heartbroken. The thought of someone finding her and keeping her for themselves creeps into the back of my mind. She's a pittie and I know people use the breed for nefarious reasons, but she's such a sweetheart. All I can do is hope the people in Asheville now aren't assholes. A lot could have changed since I lived here. Let's face it, keeping a dog without trying to find the owner is a pretty shitty thing to do.

With the basket empty, I go back inside, closing the door behind me. A quick search around the house deflates any hope Alice came home while I was outside. I hope Miles and Alexandra are having better luck.

The only left to do is wait, as useless as it feels. Pulling my phone from my pocket, I take a seat on the sofa. Maybe I can find a picture of Alice to put on social media. Not that I have very many friends from here on my list. I kind of wrote Asheville off when I moved away. I don't miss the irony in running back home when I need a fresh start. Anything to get me away from all of my ex-husband's friends and family.

I finally find a good picture of Alice to post and open up my social media app. As I'm uploading, the front door bangs open and I hear stomping.

"She's not out there," Alexandra sobs. "What if something awful happened to her?"

As much as I want to tell my sweet girl her pup will be fine, I don't. False hope isn't something I've ever given her.

"All we can do is hope someone found her and will contact us."

"Why did we have to move? It's been one thing after another." She stomps off to her room.

My brother runs a hand through his hair. "Is this a normal occurrence?"

Shrugging, I scoot over on the sofa to make room for Miles. "It depends on the day. She hasn't taken this move easily."

"I can tell." He sits down beside me, phone in his hand scrolling. "Is it because she won't see her dad?"

"Not really. She won't see her friends, and according to her it's the end of the world. But she doesn't understand all the other reasons. You remember how it was being a teenager."

He's already shaking his head. "Not really. I've partied a lot since then."

Of course that would be his response. He's definitely not the responsible sibling in the family. Well, he wasn't back then. Now he's pretty successful.

"What are you doing?" I watch his fingers move fast over his phone screen.

"Posting this picture of Alice on my social media. Alex sent me a photo. I was going to ask you do it, but the last time I checked, I was the only friend you had in the area."

"Thank you." I lean my head on his shoulder. "I had the same thought. Also, sorry this how you're bringing in the new year."

"No worries. You know I'd do anything for you and my niece. Y'all are my favorite people in the world. Peter is probably a close second."

The sound of his name warms me inside and out. I

remember following Miles and him around everywhere when we were kids. Not just because I didn't want to be left out, but also because I may have wanted to be as close to him as possible.

"Wow, we managed to beat out women for a top spot. I'm impressed."

"You should be." He grins. "Not that I have much time for dating. We've been pretty busy at the ranch."

"Can I make one request?"

My brother eyes me warily be nodding. He's never liked when I make requests of him. It usually meant taking me wherever he went because I didn't want to be home.

"Since we're back in town and Alexandra isn't used to your playboy ways, can you maybe not bring them around her unless it's something serious?"

"Callie, she's a teenager." He rolls his eyes. It's pretty much his automatic response anytime I say something he thinks is ridiculous. "She probably knows her uncle dates."

"I know, but she needs some stability right now. She hates that we moved and I don't want to do anything else that may upset her." For once I'd love for my big brother to understand where I'm coming from. It's hard because he doesn't have kids, but he should want to protect her because he's, her uncle.

He doesn't say anything for a few moments and then he leans back against the cushions. "Okay."

"Really? Just like that?"

"Do I think you're a little overprotective? Yes. But I'll respect your wishes because you're her mom. Plus, I don't want to be another reason she hates it here. Maybe I can get her to love Asheville as much as we do."

He's going a little far with the "we". If I loved it so much, I never would have left. I'll take this small victory, though. At least one thing has gone my way tonight. "Thank you."

"No problem." His grin is still like the one he used to give all the girls when we were younger. It's the one that will make you forgive him for anything. Maybe that's what it is, he's advance apology for if he screws up this one thing.

My phone vibrates in my hand. A text from an unknown number pops up.

Unknown: Hi, I think I may have found your dog. It was on Starlit Road in the field. But the address doesn't seem like a local one. Are you missing a dog?

"Oh. My. God." I screech and immediately start typing a response.

Callie: Yes. Thank you so much for finding Alice. If you send me your address we can come pick her up.

My brother is staring at me in confusion. I don't have time to explain. Our smallest family member is coming home.

The phone vibrates again.

UNKNOWN:

No need. Send me your address, and I'll bring her by.

I do as he asks and send him our address. I guess she didn't get as far as I thought she would.

"Can you please tell me what's going on?" My brother throws his hands in the air exasperated with my lack of explanation.

"Someone found Alice. They are bringing her to us now."

"I'm not leaving until they've come and gone. Let me see your phone."

Kind of a weird time for him to play the overprotective big brother, but whatever. I hand him the phone and he studies the message.

"Well, that makes me feel a bit better."

"What does?"

The fact someone found her should make him feel amazing.

"Peter is the one who found her. So, she's in good hands."

Holy shit. That's not what I was expecting. Now he's coming here. To my house. And I look terrible. If I try to change Miles will ask me why, but if I don't, I'll look like a hot mess while seeing Peter for the first time in well over a decade. Damn it.

three

. . .

peter

"ALRIGHT, Alice. You ready to go home to your family?" She's a gorgeous pittie. I'm surprised she's as small as she is, but she's lean and it's all muscle.

I'm just happy I found her owner. They must have just moved to town. The least I could do is offer to take her home. I know if she was my dog, I'd be an emotional mess. There's no use in a family getting out this late to come get their dog. It's not like I have anyone here waiting for me to get back home. It's just easier for me to do it.

Digging through my toolbox, I find a piece of rope and tie it to her collar as a makeshift leash. She may be small, but she's still heavy. The last thing I need to do is throw out my back trying to carry her again.

"Let's go girl."

Alice walks beside me as I open the door and sits while waiting for me to lock it behind us.

"Good girl." I give her a scratch behind the ear. I swear she sighs at the gesture.

She must be well trained because she doesn't try to run in front of me as we head toward my truck. She stays beside me, or slightly behind.

Maybe I should get a dog. Then I'll have something to look forward to coming home to. It'll also force me to slow down my work hours. Pierce really doesn't need me at the winery at all hours.

That's a road to cross another day. Right now, I need to get this sweet girl home to her family. I'm sure they miss her.

She jumps into the front seat of my truck with ease and I shoo her to the passenger seat. Piper would lose her mind if she saw this. Me, letting an animal into my pride and joy.

I start the truck and Alice lies down in the seat as it hums to life. There's no need to plug in the address. As soon as I saw the address, I knew exactly where this person lived. It's Beau's childhood home. He'll be glad to know it's finally sold and there's no threat of his parents coming back.

It doesn't take me long to pull into the driveway of Alice's home. Except there is a truck in the driveway I recognize.

My best friend is making his way down the sidewalk to where I'm parking and is to my truck as I open the door. "What the hell are you doing here, Miles? Did you already get friendly with the new person in town?"

It's not like it's a stretch to think it's possible. He's always been someone who can hit it off with pretty much anyone.

"Gross, dude. No." He glances behind him where a woman and what looks to be a teenager stand. "My sister moved back to town with her daughter. I thought I told you she bought this place."

"No, I feel like I would remember that." I comb through my memory to see if he did in fact tell me. And he didn't. "When did they move back?"

"Over the past week. It's why I've been so busy lately. I was making sure everything was ready for her."

"Oh, well, I guess this beautiful pup is hers?" I point my thumb over my shoulder to the dog sitting in my passenger seat.

"Yes." The sigh of relief is something I've never heard from him before. Not even when he was overprotective of his sister when we were kids. He moves to the passenger side and opens the door. "Come on, Alice. Alexandra is excited to see you." Alice jumps down with her tail wagging.

Before I have a chance to ask who Alexandra is, a girl comes running down the sidewalk and Alice breaks free from Miles. Clearly this girl is Alice's human.

"I take it this girl is Alexandra?" I really am clueless here.

"Yeah, she's, my niece. Callie's daughter."

It makes sense. I haven't seen Callie since she hightailed it out of town after graduating high school. She hasn't been back since…until now.

"Oh." It's the only thing I can think of to say.

"Come on." He slaps my shoulder. "Say hi to Callie and officially meet her daughter."

Shrugging my shoulders, I follow Miles up the sidewalk. There's nothing better to do tonight. All that awaits me at home is my video game. Plus, it'll be nice to catch up with an old friend. If I can call her that. She mostly tagged along when we were kids. We wouldn't have gotten away with half the shit we pulled if we left her behind. She always threatened to tell her parents or mine.

"Thank you so much for finding Alice." The girl, Alexandra, cries before throwing her arms around me. "I was so scared she was gone forever."

My arms are out to my side because I don't know what to do in this situation. I'm rarely around teenagers. Do I hug her back? Or stand here, awkward, until she calms down?

"It was, um, no problem." I pat her shoulder because I don't know this kid. "I'm just happy I was able to find her owners. Does she do this often?"

With one last sniffle Alexandra takes a step back. "No, we always lived in the city so there were never fireworks. I didn't think she'd react like that."

"Now you know, and you'll have that information for this summer." Shit. That sounds like I'm chastising her for something she had no control over.

"I mean, it'll help you take precautions."

Alexandra's lip quirks up in a half smile. "I knew what you meant."

Hopefully it's dark enough she doesn't see my relief. "That's good."

"I'm Alexandra." She holds out her hand to shake mine. "Apparently we're neighbors."

"I'm Peter." I give her hand a quick shake before releasing it. Are all teens like this? "I'm friends with your uncle."

"And not my mom?" Now she's crossing her arms, and I don't understand what I did wrong.

"You're mom, too. But I haven't seen her in a really long time."

Alexandra turns around and walks toward the house. I guess I'm supposed to follow her. I search for Miles for some sort of clue, but he's already at the door.

Guess I better say hi to Callie. I have a feeling if I don't her daughter will be pissed. There's no way I can do that. One because I just made her night by finding her pup. And two, it appears we're neighbors and the last thing I want to do is piss off a teen. If she's half as brazen as me and Miles were, I'm sure pranks will ensue.

I trudge up the sidewalk, several feet behind Alexandra. It's not that I have anything against Callie, but I never thought I'd see her again. She wasn't always the easiest to deal with when we were kids. Mostly because she was dead set on doing whatever me and Miles were doing.

Miles beckons me inside as soon as I'm at the front door. "Come on."

There are half empty boxes inside the room as soon as I walk in. It looks like they've made progress in unpacking. I wouldn't know. I moved from my parents' house to the house I have on Starlit Fields property. Moving is something I never had to experience.

"Callie, I'm sure you remember Peter."

She's standing in the middle of the living room, eyes wide. But I don't miss the way the travel over me from head to toe. She's not at all like I remember her. Her hair is much longer and she's not the awkward teen she was before she left. She's grown up into a beautiful woman.

"Hey." The word is raspy like she couldn't find her

voice. Not completely. "I mean hi. Sorry for the mess. We're still unpacking."

"How have you been?"

She studies me again. No doubt wondering if I'm being sincere. Her brother and I weren't always so nice to her when we were younger. Her next words are hesitant, almost like the weight of them is too much. Maybe they are. "Good. Just trying to get settled in."

"If you need any help, let me know. I'm literally right down the road." I point my thumb over my shoulder as if that will indicate the correct direction.

"I think we've got it." Miles shoots her a glare at the tone change.

Okay. That was a switch up. I'm sure she's stressed. She just moved back and had a hell of a time with her dog. I'm trying not to take it personally. Especially after dealing with all the shit with my brother.

"Well, the offer stand should you need it."

Callie takes a moment to plaster a smile on her face. It's the same fake one she wore when she told us she wouldn't tattle to our parents over something dumb Miles and I were about to do.

"Thank you. And thanks for finding Alice." The relief in the last sentence only confirms what I thought. She's trying to be strong for whatever reason. It's not really any of my business, but I'd be lying if I said I wasn't curious. "I don't know what we would have done if she was lost forever."

"It's no problem." I reassure her. "If anyone here would have found her, they would have done everything they could to find her owner. You know how the community here is."

"Yeah," she grumbles.

What the hell happened to make her dislike her home town? If it was something bad, I'm certain I would have heard about it back then. I graduated a few years before her, but word travels fast when there's something to talk about.

I'm not going to meddle. The best thing for me to do at this point is get in my truck and drive home. I returned Alice to her family. Now I can go home and start my new year off the way I intended, playing games and crashing.

"Oh, I gave her a bath after I found her. She had leaves and grass all in her fur."

"You didn't have to do that." She shakes her head. "We would have given her one as soon as we found her."

"You can just say thank you." Her eyes cut to mine. "Besides, it was a pretty rough night for the sweet girl and nobody, not even a pup, should ring in the new year without looking their best."

As soon as the words are out of my mouth, I realize it's the wrong thing to say. Callie glances down at her over-sized sweater and leggings. At least, I think that's what they're called. Piper wears them to work all the time even though Pierce tells her not to. I probably should have left that comment to myself.

"Sorry, I-I didn't mean you don't look your best. I just meant—" I don't even bother finishing the sentence. I know when I've stuck my foot in my mouth. This time I did it in such a bad way there's no redeeming myself...at least not right now.

"It's fine." I don't miss the sadness in her voice. Whatever she's going through it must be hard, and I didn't help anything by saying stupid shit at the wrong moment.

"Anyways, thank you. I'll let you know if we need anything. I'm sure you have much better things to do with your night."

I don't, but she doesn't need to know that. Hell, if it wasn't for my need to be away from people, I'd still be at the bar with my brothers and sisters. It was too much, and I needed to get out.

"I really am sorry. I didn't mean anything by what I said." I run my hand through my hair and study every empty wall in the room. Anything to not have to look her in the eye. Stupid shit just seems to flow out of my mouth at the most inopportune times.

She waves away my second attempt at an apology. "It's been a long day. Now that Alice is home, safe and sound, I kind of want to crash." Miles moves to sit on the sofa and she shoots him a glare. "You, too, Miles."

"But I thought you wanted me to help you unpack."

"I love you dearly, brother, but it's well after two in the morning. Please get out of my house."

"Fine. I'll be here bright and early in the morning since I don't have to work."

"You probably shouldn't lie to your sister." I can't help the small dig. I need someone else to feel the brunt of Callie's ire. Even if I really stepped in it.

He grins before shaking his head like he can't believe I called him out like that. "Let's get out of my sister's hair."

With a quick wave, I follow my friend out of the house. "Why didn't you tell me your sister was moving back? I could have helped with it."

"I swear I mentioned it. Anyway, she's not in a great space and will need all the support she can get it. Does your offer still stand for unpacking tomorrow?"

"Sure, I'm not doing anything else. Maybe everyone can come over for lunch at Mom and Dad's. You know they have their traditions."

"Sounds good." He opens the door to his truck and glances over. "Do I still have clothes and stuff at your house? I'm certain I've forgotten some there at some point."

"Yeah, you can crash on the couch too. It doesn't make sense for you to drive in the opposite direction to the ranch when you're coming back."

"Thanks, man." He gets into his truck and turns it on. He gives me a thumbs up before pulling out of the driveway and turning left toward my house.

I take one last glance at Callie's house. It's odd seeing her after so many years. Not too long after she moved away, I sent her a friend request on social media. She may have been annoying, but I needed to make sure she was okay in her new surroundings. It's still in the pending section.

four

. . .

callie

MY STACK of clothes is getting smaller and smaller. There's nothing quite like hearing you look like a mess to revamp the wardrobe. Seeing Peter trip over his words last night, or early this morning, was worth it. Maybe.

Since the separation I've gotten lax about my appearance. Outside of work, all I've been wearing are yoga pants and over-sized t-shirts. I guess seeing my childhood crush is the reality check I needed.

Once upon a time I cared about my appearance. It was one of the things that made me happy. Now…it feels like more work than it's worth. But moving back to Asheville is my chance to start over, and that includes my clothing choices

"I thought you said Uncle Miles was going to be here early." Alexandra is leaning against the door, Alice beside her, when I turn around.

"You're definition of early and his are two completely different things. We'll be lucky if he gets here by lunch."

Not that I blame him. He gets up early to work at the ranch, I don't blame him for wanting to sleep in when he can.

"Speaking of, what are we doing about food?" She points toward the kitchen. "We don't have much in the fridge and it's not like I can walk to the closest fast-food place. They don't have those in the middle of nowhere."

Here we go again. This is her biggest complaint about moving here. Not necessarily Asheville in general, but this house, so far away from everything. Maybe it was a mistake to move back home and upend her entire life. I mean, what high school kid wants to switch schools in the middle of the school year? But...I didn't have much of a choice. Not if I wanted a fresh start.

"I can see if your uncle will pick something up, or I'll run to town to get something for us." Those really are the only two options until I can get to the grocery store and stock up.

"Fine. I'll text Uncle Miles." The frustration in her voice isn't missed and does nothing to make me stop feeling like the worst mother in the world. "He can consider it his wakeup call."

Hopefully he's not an ass like he used to be when we were kids. I hated when our parents asked me to wake him up. The number of pillows I've had thrown at me is unreal.

"Good luck," I call to her retreating back.

The piles of clothes on my bed are judging me, and I don't want to keep separating into keep and donate piles. I wouldn't even be doing this if Peter hadn't made that comment last night. I'm blaming this all on him.

There's a yell of frustration from Alexandra and Alice starts barking. What in the world is going on out there. I rush out of the room, knocking over one of the empty boxes, and into the living room.

"Is everything okay?" My eyes study the floor and walls to see if she might have broken something.

"No," Alexandra grumbles as she points at the windows. "Uncle Miles will not be bringing food because he's already here." She takes a step closer, peering out the window. "And that guy who found Alice is with him. What's his deal anyway?"

Shit. Why did he bring Peter with him? I wasn't expecting to see him for a while. We might be neighbors, but my avoidance game is strong. I spent all of my pre-teen and teen years following him around like a puppy. I refuse to do it again as an adult.

"Mom?" Her eyebrows are raised when I glance at her. She's obviously trying to puzzle out why I'm acting weird.

Get it together, Callie. He's just a man.

"Peter and Miles have been friends since we were kids. In diapers really. They were inseparable. His family owns the winery up the road."

"Is that all? Because you look like you're about to puke."

I thought the inquiring phase ended when kids were toddlers.

"Yep. That's it."

"Hmmm." Without another word she turns and rushes out the front door to greet my brother.

I have a feeling she isn't done questioning me about

Peter, but I'm glad she's dropped it for now. The last thing I need is to tell her anything when he's in hearing distance. Besides, I don't want her to think it's healthy to pine after someone who clearly doesn't feel the same way. Back then I was a naive kid. Now…I've been let down too much to even consider any sort of relationship with anyone. Not that Peter's looking for that, of course.

It's probably best to join them so they don't think anything weird is going on with me. Alexandra is pulling from a hug with Miles as I walk outside, tucking my hands into the sleeves of my sweater to block some of the cold air.

"I guess it's too late to see if you'll bring food?" Alexandra asks him.

"Clearly." My brother rolls his eyes before coming to give me a hug. "But it would have taken me even longer since I stayed at Peter's last night."

"Why?" I don't mean for the question to come out quite so harsh.

"I had some stuff over there and figured it was easier since I was coming here this morning."

He has a point. Just because I'm here doesn't mean I get to dictate everything he does.

"Yeah, he still snores like a freaking chainsaw, too." Peter says as he closes the door.

"You're a lot less intimidating in the sunlight." Alexandra says, squinting to block said light.

"Alexandra, that's rude." My words are a hiss and she makes a face at me.

"It's fine." Peter waves the comment away. "In my defense, it was raining and gross last night. And, I've had a shower."

"So, who wants to go get food?" Alexandra looks between the three of us. "We don't have anything in there."

"I guess I could go." Miles runs his hand through his hair. "But I was hoping to get done moving the heavy stuff while I help. And getting it done early so I can get to bed at a decent time. Ranch hours aren't for the faint of heart."

"You don't have to do all that." Peter shoves his hands in his pockets. He's never been much of a speaker. He goes along with whatever anyone suggests. I blame it on his big brother.

"Why not?" Alexandra cocks her head to the side. The questions definitely didn't stop when she was a toddler. "It's not like anyone delivers out here."

"Out of the Ashes will. Perks of being business parters." He grins. "Besides if they'll deliver to Piper then they'll do it here. What do y'all like?"

There's no way we can ask him to do that. It feels like we're taking advantage of the situation. I should have done better and made sure we had some kind of food. The decision to move was made fast and I didn't have a ton of time to prepare.

"You do—" I begin, but Alexandra cuts me off.

"What kind of food do they have?"

"Really, it's fine. I can run to town and get us some food." The last thing I need is for Peter to think I'm incapable of having food in the house. I'm not the annoying tag along he remembers.

Peter levels me with a stare, and I swear everything I felt for him back then comes rushing back. It's soft and demanding at the same time. Which doesn't make sense, and I have no idea what to make of it.

"You've had a traumatic first day back with Alice. I can take care of this." He turns to my daughter to answer her question. "They have pretty much whatever you want. Except pizza. It's pretty much bar food. The wings are amazing."

"I'll have that." Alexandra grins at him before rushing back toward the house to escape the cold. "Thank you!"

"She's a good kid." Peter nods toward her. "What do you want to eat?"

"Same thing." He's going out of his way to do this thing for us, the least I can do is make my order easy for him. "Thanks."

"Any time." He smiles at me, and my heartbeat quickens.

"You aren't gonna ask what I want?" Miles throws his hands up in the air. "Go figure."

"Shut up. I know what you get."

"What if I want something different?" My brother shoots back.

I follow Alexandra inside and leave them to their bickering. At least that hasn't changed. Deep down I know I shouldn't let him do this. But damn, it feels good having someone offer to meet my needs. I rack my brain trying to remember the last time that happened, and it's been way too long.

"What are we going to unbox first?" Alexandra asks.

My feet leave the ground and I almost fall backward. She doubles over laughing because she scared me.

"It's not that funny." I grumble. "Why were you being so quiet?"

"I wasn't." She points toward the boxes on the floor.

"I've been unstacking boxes so we can figure out what goes where. Your mind must have been elsewhere."

She has a sly grin on her face, and I know that wasn't the only thing she was doing. Considering her proximity to the window, she was definitely snooping. She better not be getting any ideas about trying to set me up with Peter. Last school year she tried setting me up with a friend's dad, and it didn't work out well at all. Being a teenager is the only thing she should have on her mind, not my love life.

"Well, since we have food coming, we should probably unbox some of the kitchen stuff in case we need it." Being productive is what I need to get my mind off Peter. There's no way in hell I'm letting my past infatuation show it's face again. The only thing I need to focus on is raising my daughter and putting the pieces of my life back together.

"Sounds good." She nods and looks for one of the boxes labeled "kitchen".

Ideally, we should have unloaded the boxes in their respective rooms. The rain last night kind of killed that for us. We were too focused on getting everything inside. Then Alice ran off. The beginning of the new year has not been kind to us. Hopefully we can turn things around.

Miles and Peter join us in the living room. "The food should be here in about thirty minutes."

"How in the world is it getting here so fast?" Alexandra asks as she lifts a box.

"Eric is determined to see what's going on over here on Starlit Road. He'll be breaking every traffic law he can."

I tilt my head to the side in question. "Did we go to school with him?"

"No. He's been here a few years and has dubbed

himself the town busy body." Peter shakes his head and lifts on of the boxes. He must have noticed the label on Lexi's box. "If you don't want him in your business, it's best to say as little as possible."

"Sounds like I need to be friends with this guy." Lexi laughs and continues toward the kitchen.

I shake my head. Of course she'd want to befriend the town gossip. I guess she sees it as the only form of entertainment in Asheville. Hopefully she'll see this town has more than that to offer. Despite the drama that occurs on occasion, the community always comes together for their own.

"Eric actually has two step kids about her age. It might be a good idea to invite them over so she knows someone when she starts school," Peter says as he lifts two boxes. Show off. Also, why is he giving me parenting advice? Last time I checked his social media he was single with no kids.

"You literally just told me not to say too much to him. Now you want me to set up a play date for teens?"

"It's only an idea." He shakes his head as he makes his way to the kitchen.

Great, now I've offended him twice today.

five

. . .

peter

NO MATTER WHAT I DO, I keep saying the wrong thing. At least that's what it feels like. I don't remember her being quite so cynical when we were younger. What in the hell happened to her?

"Where should I put this?" I lift the boxes slightly higher.

Alexandra turns to see what I have, and shifts her head from side to side. "Um, the table?"

I glance over at the table, but don't see any empty spaces. "Pull out a couple of chairs."

She does it and takes a step back. "I don't know why I didn't think about putting them in the chairs. There isn't a ton of available space in here."

"Yeah, that was always an issue when Beau lived here. Though he left as soon as he could."

"Oh, you knew the people who owned this house?" She taps the top of her head as if that was a dumb question. "Of course you did. This is one of those towns where everyone knows everyone."

"Hey, don't knock the community. You never know when you might need help from someone in town." I set the boxes down and turn toward her. "But yeah, I knew the family. Well, know, them. Beau is dating my sister. But his parents were crappy so we didn't come over here all that much when we were kids. He spent most of his time at our house."

She makes a face at me and scoffs. "So, your sister is dating someone she's known practically her whole life? That's weird."

I can't help but laugh. "Yes, they've been best friends for a really long time. There were sparks from day one, but both of them were too stubborn to do anything about it until recently."

"Still weird." She shakes her and leaves the kitchen.

"You'll have to forgive her rudeness." Callie comes into the kitchen and stands as far away from me as possible. Do I smell or something? Considering she was by mine and Miles's side our entire childhood, this distance feels odd. "She seems to have forgotten how she was raised."

"Teens will be teens…I guess." Not that I would know. I'm really not around that many teenagers unless one of my siblings finds a way to drag me to one their friends' get togethers.

"Yeah, it's definitely been an adjustment. Most days I don't know which version of Lexi I'm going to get." A small smile tugs at the corner of her mouth. "Thank you for helping today."

"It's not a problem. If I didn't come here, I probably would have found something to do at the winery. It's gotten busy since Piper has taken over all social media for us. Plus, she's putting together these events with Paula."

Dear God, I'm rambling. So, I say the wrong thing, give unsolicited advice, or talk for long periods of time when I'm around her. What is wrong with me?

"It's good to hear that. I'm sure your grandparents are proud."

"They, uh, passed away a few years ago."

"Shit. I'm sorry." Her eyes move to floor. "I didn't realize. Guess I've done a shitty job of keeping up with everyone here."

The way she says it makes my heart hurt. Like she's beating herself up for not knowing what's going on in my life. "It's okay. It's not like you've been around. You had a life you were living."

She snorts at the comment. "If you want to call it that."

Nope. I'm not going to open that can of worms. This is the year I'm focusing on myself. I can't jump into the problems of a pretty woman I once knew. I'm not sure how long she's been divorced, but it sounds like the wounds are still fresh.

Though, I figured Miles would have mentioned it at some point. Unless they have those super tight secrets most siblings have. There are things about some of my brothers I wish I never knew.

"Is whatever happened why you moved back?" So much for not sticking my nose where it belongs.

"In part, but I don't really want to talk about it."

The relief that floods through me probably doesn't speak well of me as a person, but I don't like heavy topics. I'm the person who gets things done and does what people tell me. Which is one of the things Piper wants me to work on. This would be a great opportunity for it, but I don't have the energy for it.

My phone vibrates in my pocket. "It looks like Eric is almost here. I'll meet him outside so he doesn't snoop too much."

"It's fine. Your idea about bringing his kids around is a good one. I might as well meet him with you."

She heads toward the entryway ahead of me and I follow her. She doesn't grab a jacket or anything despite the cold. Little does she know, Eric is a yapper. I shrug out of my jacket and carry it with me as I follow her out of the house.

Eric is pulling into the driveway as we meet the end of the sidewalk. Before Callie has a chance to argue, I slide my jacket over her shoulders.

"I don't really need this. We aren't going to be out here that long...are we?"

"You never really know with Eric. I guess it depends how badly they need him at the bar."

"Why would that matter?"

"He's the head bartender."

"Oh. What happened to Angie?"

Wow, she really needs someone to bring her up to speed with everything that's gone on in Asheville since she left all those years ago. "She owns it now. I'll fill in the gaps while we eat lunch. I'm surprised Miles hasn't done it."

"We didn't talk much about Asheville when he called or visited."

That's...odd. It's not something I'll get to the bottom of in one day. The urge to know what made her run off and not look back is a battle I won't win for long. So much for not caring.

Eric parks in front of the house and we move to meet him at his car. It's best not to give him a chance to come inside. Not today at least.

"Hey, man." He wraps me in a hug. "I saw you left early last night. Do we not throw a good enough party for you?"

I disentangle myself from him. He knows I'm not a hugger and he does it to get under my skin. It's like he finds out what annoys you and does it anyway.

"You know damn well big parties aren't my thing." I take a step back. "Besides, I told my sister I was leaving and I had her blessing."

Eric waves away my confession. I swear he takes it as a personal affront if I leave a function earlier than he wishes. He's not even the one who was throwing the party it was the bar as a whole.

"So, who is the newest addition to the good town of Asheville?" He glances over at Callie and holds his hand out, waiting for her to do the same.

"She's not actually new. It's more of like a return to home." I offer so he doesn't make an ass of himself. Not that he would care. Honestly, I'm not sure how people go through life like that. No caring what people think, or expect, of you. Maybe he should be the one helping me reinvent myself.

"Oh, even better." Eric laughs. "I'm Eric. I'm head bartender at Out of the Ashes."

"Callie." She shakes his hand and gives him a small smile. "I'm Miles's sister and basically doing the walk of shame for having to come back home."

"There's nothing wrong about coming back to family." The words are out of my mouth before I can stop them. So maybe I'm a little upset she abandoned us all those years ago. As frustrating as it was hauling her around everywhere when we were teens, the silence was worst.

"I never said that." Callie bites back. "You have no idea how grateful I am to Miles for helping me out when I needed it most."

Eric's eyes widen as he removes his hand from Callie's. I—is that a smirk? This jerk is getting enjoyment out of it. As long as he doesn't try to do his whole match-making thing I keep hearing about. That's the last freaking thing I need.

"I'm just gonna get your food." He moves toward his car with a quickness I've never seen before. Any other time he's itching to stick around.

I wonder what has him scurrying away. Then I see Callie's face. Her scowl is one I remember seeing from our childhood. Nothing good ever followed it.

"I didn't mean it like that." The need to diffuse the situation is more important than ever. The last thing I need is for Eric to see her full temper, especially when it's directed at me. I'm pretty sure I'm his least favorite Summers kid aside from Pierce.

"How else am I supposed to take it?" She crosses her arms over chest. I know she's trying to be intimidating but it's actually adorable.

"All I'm saying is you left town and never looked back. It's like you dropped off the face of the earth and our little town didn't mean shit to you anymore."

Instead of arguing with me like I expect her to, she

starts laughing. "Geez, Peter, I didn't know you cared so much."

"I don't."

This time it's Eric chuckling. "I'm gonna head out, we're sure to hit the normal rush now that everyone is waking up from their hangovers. Here's your food." He hands me two bags and Callie one.

"Wouldn't a bar be the last place you want to go after a hangover?" Callie tilts her head to the side.

"Hair of the dog," Eric grins. "You should come by and see us once you're settled."

"Yeah, sure."

The tone of her voice means she's not going to. I can't help but wonder when she last went out and enjoyed herself. Not that I can judge. My idea of a good time is hanging out at home playing video games or working at the winery. Very rarely do I venture outside of that routine. Except…last night. Maybe I should be glad I went out. Otherwise, I wouldn't have known Callie moved in practically next door until Miles deemed it important enough to mention. Not that it matters.

"Thanks, Eric." I give him a small wave. "I'll come by for lunch this week."

"I'm holding you to that." He lifts his hand as he turns to his car. Within seconds he's backing out and on his way.

"He's not as scary as you made him seem." Callie frowns at me and carries her bag inside.

That's not even what I said. He's nosy, not scary. I honestly don't know if he has a mean bone in his body. He's more like a golden retriever that likes to know everyone's business. Maybe that's how I should have described him to her.

"Just wait until he gets all in your business." I mutter under my breath.

"Which is why I don't plan on going to the bar. Not for a long while."

What the hell? I could barely hear myself.

"How did you know what I said?"

She taps her finger against the side of her head. "Mom ears. We hear everything."

Huh, I always thought that was a myth. It must be some superpower people get when they have kids. "You realize that's creepy, right?"

"Alexandra thinks the same thing." She shrugs and motions for me to put the bags on the coffee table in the living room. "I'll grab the other two if you want to start pulling things out of the bags."

"Sure." I watch her leave the room and do as she requested. She already has to parent one person, I don't need to give her another one.

Callie being back is odd. We've gone so many years without her here and now she shows up. Based on our interactions so far, we're going back to the same relationship we had when we were kids. This whole thing is about to get interesting.

six

. . .

callie

ASHEVILLE SEEMS the same as it did when I lived here all those years ago. It does seem like the community has gotten younger. Or maybe I'm at an age now where I fit in with the older folks who ran the town when I was a kid.

The one thing that hasn't changed is the willingness of the community to offer support. They welcomed me back with open arms. Job offers have been rolling in. I'm not even sure if some of the positions exist, but it's the thought that counts. I will need to find something soon. My savings account will only get us so far.

"Lexi, are you ready?"

It's her first day at Asheville High School, and she's in for a major change. Even with population growth for the town, it's still much smaller than what she's used to. I only hope she doesn't hate me for moving her here. She may be old enough to understand the reason, but she won't hear it from me. I refuse to talk badly about her dad, and his side of the family, no matter how horrible they are.

"Almost." She yells from her room.

It's probably a good thing I'm taking her to school. At least, until I see what kind of job I find. She'll never be able to get up early enough to take the bus. She likes her sleep way too much. Things will be easier once she gets her license. Which reminds me, I need to see about enrolling her in a driving school. I open up my phone and add it to the ever-growing to-do list.

"You're going to be late." It's a gentle reminder, but I'm sure I'll get some type of mood with her response.

She walks from the hallway with her backpack hanging over her shoulder. "Sorry, I couldn't find my jeans and my hair is doing weird things. Can I just not go and try again tomorrow?"

The pleading in her eyes is almost laughable. It's even funnier she thinks I'll let that fly. "Nice try, kid. Let's go."

"Fine," she grumbles and follows me out the front door. "Hold on."

She runs back to her room and I continue on my way. I should have gotten the car started earlier, but I didn't want to waste gas.

As I turn on the car, I watch Alexandra close the door and press the button to lock it. I'm not entirely sure that's needed out here. We lived in town growing up and we never locked the doors. She grew up in more heavily populated area and it's a habit at this point.

She runs to the car, opens the door and jumps into the passenger seat. "It's freezing out here."

"That's typically what happens in Winter. What did you forget?"

She holds up a black bundle of fabric. "My hoodie."

"And you didn't think to put it on before walking out of the house?"

"You told me to hurry." She rolls her eyes and buckles her seatbelt. After shoving her backpack to the floor, she pushes the seatbelt behind her to put on the hoodie. After a few seconds she repositions her seatbelt and grins at me. "I'm ready now."

It's cute she thinks she runs this show. Although, some days it feels like it. She's been through a lot in the last two years and I probably let her get away with more than I should. My parents would freak out if they knew how much. I guess they'll find out when they come back to town and visit. It must be nice living that retired life.

I pull out of the driveway and begin the long trek to town. It's really only fifteen minutes, but it was less than that to walk to Lexi's old school. Living here will be an adjustment for the both of us, even though I grew up here. It's been too long since I lived in an area where we have to go to town to get any sort of necessities.

"When we get there, I'll drop you off at the front of the school. Go straight to the office. They should have your schedule ready."

For a split second I notice her uncertainty. She may put on a brave face, but there's fear beneath it. "What if I hate it here?"

I hate the quiver in her voice, and I wish we could have stayed in Oklahoma. But it wasn't healthy for either of us. One day she'll realize this was the best course of action.

"There's always homeschool." I do my best to joke about it in hopes of it easing her fear.

"Absolutely not." She shakes her head and I can see a

slight grin pass her face. "No offense, but you're not a great teacher. Remember when you were trying to show me how to ride a bike?"

"Geez, did you have to bring that up?" It was a disaster. She kept turning the bike into me and I had a hard time explaining the brake situation to her. It did not go well.

"I mean, you're the one who suggested homeschool. Just thought I should remind you of your lack of teaching skills."

"Noted." We're coming into town and the donut shop seems to be empty. Or as empty as I've ever seen it right before school. "Want some breakfast?"

At first, I think she's going to pass on the offer. But she glances over at me and nods. "Actually, I think that's a good idea. And if I get super nervous and puke, I'll get to go home."

"That's an odd way of looking at it, but okay."

Within minutes Lexi has her breakfast and she's eating as we continue to the high school. When I pull in front of it her eyes widen.

"Why is it so big? This town is tiny."

"They had to build a new one because folks are moving here for the slower pace of life." I pull up to the front door and put the car in park. "I can go in with you if you want me to. Like I said everything should be ready to go, but if you want moral support, I can do that, too."

She shakes her head and scoffs. "Because that's how I want my first impression to go. Everyone will think I need my mom to handle everything for me." She takes a deep breath and reaches for the door. "I can do this."

"Yes, you can." I reach over and give her a quick hug.

"By the end of the week, you'll be running this place. Have a good day. Love you."

She opens the door and steps out. But before she closes it, she leans in and smirks. "You have way too much faith in me when it comes to making friends. I'll make the best of it. Love you, too."

Before I have a chance to argue, she closes the door and walks to the school. Her steps are slow and I know she's dreading it, but she'll find her footing. I wait until she's inside before putting the car in drive and pulling away. This may be almost as hard as it was dropping her off on the first day of kindergarten.

It will take everything in my power not to check on her every thirty minutes. To keep myself occupied, I head toward the library. At least I can look through some of these job offers in peace. It's also the one place that brought me joy when I was a kid. None of the other people my age ventured there, and it meant I didn't get picked on by the popular kids.

"Oh my God, is that you, Callie?" Angie shrieks and rushes from around the bar to wrap her arms around me. "Long time no see."

"Hey, Angie." I disentangle myself from her and study Out of the Ashes. It's a lot different than it used to look. I remember tagging along with my brother when Angie's uncle would let us hang out here. He'd close the place down just for us. "Things sure look a lot different around here."

She moves to my right and a huge smile overtakes her

face. "I know. I think Uncle Max would be proud. The bar is a lot different than when he ran it. I had a lot of help, though."

"It looks great. From what Miles says, this is the place to be."

"For the most part. Now that Starlit Fields has started doing events, people have more choices."

"I didn't realize they'd gotten so big."

She laughs. "You really have been away for far too long. Let's get a bite to eat and catch up, my treat."

I wave my hands in the air. "You don't need to do that, I'm sure you're busy."

"Nonsense." She grabs a menu and nods her head toward the other side of the room. "Think of it as a welcome home meal."

Angie has always been generous and I know arguing with her won't help anything. She won't let me leave until I've eaten. Hell, her brother's the whole reason my brother has a job. If it wasn't for the ranch, I don't know that Miles would have made the best decisions.

"Okay." I follow her to a table tucked away in a corner. "I hope I'm not keeping you from your customers."

"You're not." She glances over her shoulder to make sure nobody needs anything. "I have a pretty great team working with me. Between Carlos and Eric, I don't even need to be here half the time, but I like working."

"Oh, I met Eric the other day."

Her eyes widen. Though, I don't think it's out of shock. Maybe in how the interaction went. "I bet that was an experience. Sorry for however he may have offended you. I take responsibility for him as his employer."

"He was perfectly nice. Everyone keeps telling me I

should watch myself around him, but I didn't see any red flags."

She nods toward the menu for me to look over. "Give it time. He really has the best of intentions. He just thinks he has to know everyone's business." She taps her chin, lost in thought. "Actually, I think he's given input on a lot of my friend's relationship problems and they've all managed to have healthy, strong outcomes."

Those words stop my menu perusal. "Oh, no. I'm not interested in any relationships. It's actually the last thing I need in my life right now."

A server comes to take our order keeping whatever Angie was about to say at bay. I give my order, pretty much what Peter picked out for me the other day. He wasn't wrong, the wings are delicious and I bet they taste even better when they are fresh from the kitchen and not being delivered.

Moments later the server sets down two glasses of sweet tea. I unwrap the straw and place it inside the glass before taking a drink.

"I guess this means you're done following Peter around like you did when we were kids."

Now I'm choking. Angie gets up and pats me on the back until my coughing is under control. I swear to God she waited for that exact moment to pose the question.

"You good?" She asks. At my nod she moves back to her chair.

"You make it sound like I was some sort of lovesick puppy."

"Weren't you, though?" She shakes her head. "I'm mostly shocked he and your brother never picked up on it."

"It was merely a childhood crush." I close my mouth as the server sets our food on the table and quickly backs away. "One that is completely gone." Maybe if I say it enough, it'll be true. "Besides, dating isn't even on my radar. And when I decide to put myself out there, I have some requirements."

"This should be good." Angie grins, waiting to see what I have to say. Even though she's the same age as Miles and Peter, she's always treated me like a friend. She never looked at me as the annoying little sister.

I pick up a wing and dip it in ranch before taking a bite. Anything to delay my response. It doesn't help. Her arms are crossed on top of the table, and she is laser focused on me.

"I'd prefer for them to have at least one child."

"Why? That seems like the exact opposite of what most people want."

Spoken as someone who doesn't have kids. "Because they know the struggle of being a single parent, and won't get mad if I end up having to shift plans around."

She nods. I'm glad she gets it. "What else?"

"I don't want them to be someone we grew up with."

"You realize most people never leave this town, or they do and come back." She waves her hand in my direction to prove her point. "So that may be harder, but there are new people coming to Asheville for a taste of that small town life."

"Which is just as well." I shrug and take another bite. "I have enough to worry about with getting Alexandra settled and finding a job."

"True enough." She agrees. "Is she riding the bus home from school?"

"Nope. I'm picking her up. I don't want to throw too much at her with it being her first day."

Angie glances at the clock on the wall. "Well, you may want to leave in the next fifteen minutes. There's nothing that creates a traffic jam in town quite like the school pick up line."

Crap. I didn't even think about that. "Thanks."

We spend the rest of the time finishing our meals and laughing about all the shenanigans we used to get into as kids. As happy as I was to leave all those years ago, I'm glad to be back. The way she picks up like nothing ever changed is exactly what I needed in my life.

"Lunch was good. You've really done something amazing here." I wave my hand to encompass the bar. "I'll definitely be back."

We both slide out of our chairs and give each other a quick hug.

"You better. And good luck with all your stipulations when you're ready to date again."

"That'll be a long time."

Little does she know, I came up with those rules because they exclude Peter. I can't fall back into my old habits.

seven

. . .

peter

"WE'RE MOST likely closing early today."

I drop the log in my hand at the sound of Piper's voice. She has always managed to scare the hell out of me without meaning to. It's one of her superpowers. Though, I guess she had to develop something as the baby of the family when we didn't immediately include her in things.

"Why?" Bending over, I pick up the log and move it to the stack next to the fireplace. One day I need to talk Pierce into converting this to gas. It has to be easier to manage than having to get firewood. We only ever use it during the winter. The sad thing is it's not even to provide warmth. Piper said it adds to the cozy atmosphere when people come in for tastings. For that we can play crackling fire on the TV without heating up the whole house.

She sits on one of the sofa's close to the fireplace. "I'm not sure. Pierce said something about a Winter storm. The roads are supposed to get bad."

"None of us even travel down the roads." We all live on Starlit Fields property. Our parents gave each of us our own lots to build a house. "Closing early is kind of pointless."

She scoffs. "I thought you were going to stop working so much and focus on yourself. Or was that resolution a complete lie to get me off your back?"

"It wasn't a lie, but there's nothing for me to do at home besides watch TV and play games." And think about Callie, but I'm not telling my sister that bit of information. She'll be as bad as Eric trying to play matchmaker. Except I haven't been able to get her off my mind since I helped unpack her boxes. It felt like she was purposely pushing me away.

"What about Miles? I'm sure he might want to hang out."

"If there really is a storm coming, he won't be able to leave the ranch. Plus, it's on the other side of town. Do you really want him risking his life to amuse me?"

Now she's outright laughing. Did I just hear her slap her knee?

"Please. I guess I need to remind you of all the dumb shit the two of you used to do when you were younger."

Oh God. She would bring up stuff from my past to rub it in my face. "Absolutely not." I finish arranging the wood and sit down next to her. "What are you going to do if we end up closing?"

Piper shrugs. "I don't know. Probably watch romcoms with Beau. Play card games. You know, the usual storm activities."

"Mind if I crash?"

"Absolutely not. The more the merrier." She pauses for

a second. "Except Pierce. We do not need his grumpy, bossy ass to make us miserable. We deal with that enough here."

Here we go again. He's not my favorite person either, but maybe it's because some of us purposefully shut him out. "He's not all that bad."

"Uh uh." She wags her finger in front of my face. "We are not going down the road where you defend Pierce like a good little lap dog. You're done with that, remember?"

"How is listening to you tell me what to do any different?"

I'm not like the rest of the siblings, I don't have a favorite. Well, not anymore. Pierce used to be that to me. I looked up to him. Did everything I could to impress him and try to earn his respect. Where did that get me? Nowhere. The secrets he kept last year about Mom and Dad were too much. Their retirement shouldn't have been a secret from any of us. Then the crap he pulled on Piper was the last straw. While I don't loathe him as much as the rest of my brothers and sisters do, the whole ordeal was eye opening to say the least.

"I guess it's not." She crosses her arms over her chest the same way she did when we were kids. "Fine, if you want to invite him, do it. But don't get mad if I'm frosty toward him."

Without missing a beat she busts out laughing.

"What's so funny?"

"Get it? Frosty? We're getting a winter storm. I swear that wasn't on purpose."

Shaking my head, I stand up. If we really are closing early, there are some things I need to finish up. "Sorry to tell ya, little sister, but if you have to explain the joke…it's not that funny."

She lifts a pillow and aims it toward me before thinking better of it. She sets it back down and scowls at me. "You better be glad there are multiple breakable things in this room. Otherwise, I would have taken you out."

"If you're feeling froggy." I chuckle, but pick up my pace to leave the building the second she starts to stand.

The air does seem colder as I step outside. At least a few degrees from when I brought in the firewood. Maybe Piper's right and we really are getting a winter storm. It's not unusual for our area, but it's not my favorite.

I pull out my phone to check the weather as I make my way to the building where we bottle the wine. Sure enough, a big red banner pops up over our area. Maybe Piper is right. I know our big brother doesn't like to chance people getting out in horrible conditions if they don't have to.

Well, the plus side is folks will have already chilled bottles of wine. Especially if the power doesn't hold up during this storm. I don't have much faith since we lost power in the Fall from a thunderstorm.

I get the workstations clear off. There's no use in them being a mess when we come back to work tomorrow. Though, if it gets as bad as my brother seems to think it is, we may be off for a couple of days. If there's one thing we hate, it's driving on ice. That seems to be all we get in our area when it's cold. It'd be nice if we got actual snow for once.

What am I even thinking? I hate the cold. Not that it's all bad. It would provide the perfect cuddling weather. That is, if I had someone to cuddle with. But I don't. Dates are hit and miss for me. Mostly because of my brother. If he needs me to do anything I typically cancel my plans and take care of what he's asked.

Piper is definitely right. I need to stop bending to his will. He's capable of doing half the crap I do. The only reason he doesn't is because he knows I'll handle it.

From now on I'm putting my foot down. Unless it's something that directly relates to my job, Pierce can handle it himself. Or, pass it off to one of the other siblings, which is what he will likely do. I need to start living for once, and stop calling off dates because of some small shit apparently only I can take care of. I'm leaning into the resolution Piper gave me. If I don't, I'll be miserable. The last thing I want is to grow old with nobody to share my life with, or have any regrets.

"Wrap up with whatever you're doing. We're closing in a hour." Speak of the devil.

"Okay. I'm just cleaning up a bit." I don't know why I feel the need to explain what I'm doing when he can clearly see.

"I'll be staying here through the storm just in case anything goes wrong. We don't need another roof debacle like the one last year." Pierce pins me down with a stare. "You're more than welcome to stay."

The way he says that rubs me the wrong way. It's like a gentle command. A part of me wants to agree to it in order to please my big brother, but no. I can't do that. I told Piper I was going to do what I want for me. Besides, I'm sure I'd have way more fun at her house before I head home.

"Actually, I think I'm going to head home."

My refusal takes him by surprise, and he shakes his

head in confusion. "If you change your mind I'm here. Don't forget to have your generator ready in case the power goes out."

The urge to say yes, Dad bubbles up, but I don't. The last thing I want to do is get an argument with him. "I always have it ready. The weather is too unpredictable."

"Good." He turns back toward the door. "I'll let everyone else know. Don't worry about staying the full hour. You can head out whenever you're done."

I love my brother, I do. But he doesn't have to sound so gruff when he gives information. Maybe one day he'll realize that a lot of the time it's not what he says to us that makes us frustrated with him, but how he says it. The tone makes all the difference.

I finish putting away the empty bottles and wiping down countertops. Another quick glance around the room, and I can finally go home. Well, go to the house before I head over to Piper's. As much as I would like to invite the other siblings, it'll be loud and I'd just rather not.

"You headed straight to my house?" Piper is standing outside the packing building when I open the door.

"Do you have a sixth sense about where I'm at?"

"Nope." She shakes her head and glances around to make sure she wasn't overheard. "This is usually where you come to tidy up when you don't want to be bothered by anyone else. It's like organizing is your super power."

"It's really not." I lock the door before closing it behind me. "But, I'm gonna head home first. I was planning on making deer chili tonight for dinner. I'll bring all the ingredients over to your house and make it there."

"Sounds like a plan." She grins as she walks next to me the main house, and follows me into office. "Your chili is the best. But, if you plan on taking any home, you may want to bring some storage bowls. Oh, and probably the things you need to cook it."

I roll my eyes. "One of these days you'll have to buy grown up things for your house, little sister. Maybe that's what I'll get you for the next holiday."

"God no." I wish I had a camera to capture the horror on her face right now. "Why would you get me a boring gift? You know damn well I don't cook."

"Ah, to be young again." I laugh. "You better watch yourself. One day you'll be excited about getting appliances and a new kitchenware."

"I hope not." She turns off the computer, grabs her bag, and has her hand on the light switch. "Now, go home, get all the things, and come to the house. I already know the first game we're playing."

Deep in my gut I know she's thinking of one I hate. She likes to annoy the hell out of me like that. I'm actually not big on any kind of games because so many of my siblings' cheat and don't follow the rules. We've gotten into actual fights over it. The life of six kids is never boring.

"I'll be over there as soon as I get the stuff. Please don't make me walk into anything embarrassing."

"The fact you even think I would risk it is hilarious. The last thing I want my brother to see is me having sex."

I throw my hands over my ears as she turns off the light. "Please never mutter the word sex in relation to you ever again."

She laughs all the way to the front door and walks out. I swear my sister knows exactly how to get under my skin. Going over there tonight will either be a great idea or a bad one. I guess I'll find out soon.

eight

. . .

callie

WHY IS IT SO COLD? I thought the further South I moved, the warmer it would be. I'm sitting in the car waiting on the school to release Alexandra. We got an alert that there would be early dismissal. This storm is supposed to be pretty bad. At least, that's what all the reports say. But really, all we ever got down here was ice. How bad can it really be?

Could Lexi have ridden the bus? Yes. Am I too much of a mama bear to let that happen? Also, yes. There's no point in having the bus come down our road when she's the only person who gets off there. Maybe it'll allow the driver to get the kids home slightly earlier, and get themself home to their family.

My phone rings and I answer without seeing who it is. Not many people from my prior life reach out anymore. Once I left, they forgot I existed. I guess it shows who my true friends are. I think I've talked to Angie more than anyone I've spent the last sixteen years with.

"Hello?"

"Cal, are you home?" Miles doesn't bother with a greeting.

"I'm at the school waiting on Lexi. What's up?"

"Just wanted to make sure you were home before this storm. You have groceries and all that, right?"

Do I? I went grocery shopping a couple of days ago, but I never buy a ton at a time. It's just me and Alexandra. We don't require much.

"Yeah, I have some food. Why?"

"Good. At least you're prepared. If things go wild with this storm, I wanted to be sure you have everything you need. I won't be able to leave the ranch."

"I've managed storms without you for quite a while. We'll be fine."

"I know. I know." He chuckles and is silent for a bit. "It's hard not being an overbearing brother. I'm trying to stop, but it's difficult now that you're only fifteen minutes away."

He's not wrong. He still tried to be protective when I was living in Oklahoma, but it's not like he could take his lunch time to come check on me when he thought I was lying to him. Which I was most of the time. Things weren't great, but I did my best to pretend I had the picture-perfect life for him.

"All I'm saying is if I move away again, it'll be your fault."

"That's not funny." Someone calls his name in the background, and I have a feeling he's not supposed to be on the phone with me. "I have to go. But call me if you need anything and I'll do my best to get over there. I can't make any promises, though."

"We'll be fine. Stop worrying."

"Okay. Love ya little sister."

I roll my eyes. I don't know why he says it like that. Maybe it's to remind me he thinks it's his job to take care of me. It's annoying, but I'll let it slide.

"Love you, too, Miles. Now get back to work."

I end the call before he can come back with a smartass comment. Kids are hurrying out of the school as I put my phone in the cupholder. None of them are my daughter, though. Hopefully Lexi checks her phone before getting on the bus. Otherwise, this will be a wasted trip.

Finally, I see her come through the doors. She glances around for my car and makes a dash for me as soon as she sees me.

A blast of cold air comes in as she opens the door and throws her bag in the floorboard. "Why can't it be Spring yet?"

"Because it's January?" I grin at the disdain on her face. "How was your day at school?"

"Okay, I guess. There isn't much we can do when it's freezing outside and end the day earlier than expected."

"At least you get the rest of the day off school." I shrug and put the car in drive. I have a feeling the traffic is going to be worse than normal. "Miles called and is worried we aren't prepared for this storm."

"That figures." She puts her seatbelt on and turns the air vents to point directly at her. She probably wouldn't be so cold if she'd wear something other than a hoodie. "We are prepared, right?"

"Yes. As much as we can be. It's not like I can control what the weather does." Though, it'd be really cool if I did. Like the character in the cartoons, I watched as a kid. I'd probably make it Fall weather all the time, though. Well, a normal fall season. Not like what we have in Texas.

"Good. I plan on cuddling up in my bed with Alice and reading."

"After you do your chores, of course."

She sighs, loudly. "Yes, after I do my chores."

"Sounds like a plan. Maybe we can watch a movie tonight. If the weather prediction is so bad you have early dismissal, I doubt you'll have school tomorrow."

"That's a good point. A movie night and sleeping in tomorrow. That is the dream life."

It really is. We have to get home first, though.

Ice crackles as I pry the door open to let Alice outside to potty. She was in my face bright and early this morning. She's not going to be happy when she steps one paw outside. Maybe I should get her some of those puppy shoes for when it's cold like this. I bet she'd appreciate it.

She takes one step onto the porch and looks back at me before trying to come back inside. "Sorry, pup. You need to go potty first."

When she realizes I'm not going to let her in after a few moments. She hurries to the yard to take care of business. The whole yard is bright white. It's almost blinding.

The sleet started while we were watching the movie. I didn't realize it turned into snow overnight. Large flakes are still falling to the ground. If this keeps up, they won't have school for another day or two.

"Mom, close the door. It's freezing in here."

"I thought you were sleeping in."

Alexandra wraps her comforter around her body. "I thought I was too. I guess I'm used to my school schedule now. This sucks."

"At least you're not in school."

"Point taken." She glances in the yard. "We're totally building a tiny snowman after we eat breakfast. I didn't think it snowed in Texas."

"It doesn't. At least, not often." Alice rushes inside almost knocking Alexandra over. I close the door and turn to my daughter, doing my best to hold the giggle bubbling up. "Help me with breakfast? You'll be warm."

"Just so you know, I'm only doing the easy stuff." She turns and heads straight to the kitchen. "You didn't have to laugh." The last words are muttered, but it's loud enough for me to hear.

Now, I feel bad. Sort of. She definitely needs more sleep because she's more in her emotions when she doesn't have get her full eight hours.

"Go cuddle up under the covers." I say as I enter the kitchen a few moments after her. "I'll handle breakfast."

"Thanks." She doesn't wait to see if I'll change my mind and hightails it to her room. I don't blame her. The adjustment has been fairly easy for her, but I can tell she misses her friends. Hopefully she'll make new ones as the year progresses.

Right now, though, the most important thing I need to do is cook. It is cold in here, and it feels like the temperature is dropping. Which is wild since you'd think it would get warmer as the sun comes up.

Small taps can be heard hitting the windows as I turn on the oven to make biscuits. I guess the sun is going away and we're getting more sleet. Maybe this storm is going to be bad as the weather folks said. I just hope nothing catastrophic happens before it's done.

"Mom, my phone is dead." Lexi calls from my bedroom door.

"Put it on the charger."

"I already tried that, but it's not working. The power is out."

Those four words have me sitting up in my bed. "Do you know how long it's been out?"

I glance over at her, and she is bundled up more than she was yesterday morning. Is she wearing a hat?

"Nope. But I'm guessing a couple of hours."

"You know you could have led with that instead of your phone being dead." I reach over to my nightstand to grab my phone.

"Yours is also dead." Her eyes are focused on anything but me.

"Why is that?"

I don't have a problem with her being on my phone, but at least let me know.

"Because I was trying to watch a show in bed while mine was charging and I fell asleep."

Now I can't contact the electric company. If we're having power issues, I'm sure everyone else is, too.

"Grab my keys and plug them up in the car."

She nods and dashes to the front of the house. I throw my comforter off and the second my body meets the air, I shiver. No wonder she's wearing so many layers. It's freezing in here.

Hurrying over to my dresser, I grab a pair of sweatpants to slide over my yoga pants and the thickest pair of socks I own. Next is an oversized sweater. We definitely need to let the power company know we don't have electricity.

As I step outside my bedroom, I close the door. I move along the rest of the house closing doors. It's the only way we'll be able to keep any sort of heat contained to one room. If I had the number of blankets my parents did, I would block off sections of the house.

"Um, we have a visitor." Alexandra says as I make my way into the living room. Peter is standing next to her.

I do my best to cover the shock on my face, but also curse at my luck. Of course, he'd show up when I just roll out of bed. I comb my fingers through my hair, doing my best to tame it.

"W-what are you doing here?" I hate the way I stutter when he's around. After all this time, this man should not have this effect on me.

He shoves his hands in his pockets and rocks back and forth on his feet. "Your brother couldn't get ahold of you. He asked me to check on y'all since he can't leave the ranch."

Figures. Miles worries way too much. I don't miss the way Lexi slips out of the room. "Our phones died. But, as you can see, we are both alive and well."

"Except you don't have power."

"How do you know that?" Sun streams in through the windows so it's not like we would have the lights on in the first place.

"The smoke detectors are beeping."

As soon as he says it, I hear the high-pitched sound. I'm surprised Alice isn't losing her mind. It's one of those loud noises she doesn't like. Not that I blame her. It's more annoying than anything else.

"Add water to the things that aren't working." Lexi comes back to the living room with an empty glass in her hand.

Peter doesn't even wait for a response from me. He heads to the kitchen and I follow behind him. He turns the handle on the sink faucet, and sure enough…nothing comes out. I could have sworn I left it dripping last night.

He pushes the handle back into position and turns to face me. "You should probably pack a bag."

"Why?"

"Because you and Alexander are coming to stay with me."

Teenage me would have jumped at this. Not now, though. I'm older, wiser, and capable of thinking about things other than how this man used to make me feel.

"No. We're. Not." I refuse to let him dictate what I'm going to do in my own house. "We have Alice to think about, and we'll be fine here. This weather shouldn't last too much longer."

"Alice can come, too. I'm not going to let the pup freeze in this house on her own." A flash of hurt crosses his face at the insinuation he wouldn't let her come.

"That's all fine and well, but if we don't have power, I highly doubt you do." His family may be well off, but it's not like they have their own piece of the grid where the power never goes out.

"I don't." I open my mouth to argue my point, but he holds up his finger. "I have a generator and a fireplace. And…running water."

"I'm in." Lexi says before dashing out of the kitchen. If I know her, she's going to pack because in her mind, this is settled.

"We can't intrude on you like that. I'm sure you have other things going on."

At this point I'll say anything to keep from being cooped up in a house with nowhere to run when my past emotions try to bubble up.

He shakes his head, and if I'm not mistaken, he's trying to hide a grin.

"The winery is closed until the roads clear up. I can take you to the ranch to stay with Miles, but he doesn't have room for all of you. I have a spare bedroom, warmth, and anything else you might need." He runs a hand through his short hair. "Please don't fight me on this. Otherwise, I'll pack up my generator and do what I can here."

Oh, hell no. He's not inviting himself to stay at my house. I know he means well, but I'm grown. Why can't my brother, or Peter for that matter, understand that? However, I know this is a losing battle. Especially since my child is already getting ready.

"Fine. But I don't think my car will make it on these roads." I know it won't. The tires need to be replaced and there's no way I'm chancing that drive with my kid.

"That's fine. There's room in my truck." He glances

around the kitchen. "Is there anything you need me to grab while you get a bag?"

"Alice's bed and some of her toys. She needs to be comfortable while we're away from home."

"I can handle that. Take as long as you need."

"Okay." It won't take me long. I don't plan on taking much except for comfy clothes. Anything to remind myself that I'm not dating anyone anytime soon. Especially him.

nine

. . .

peter

WHAT THE FUCK am I thinking? All Miles said to do is check on them. Make sure they are okay. Not draw a line in the sand tell them to stay with me. It's a bad idea. I knew as soon as the words fell from my mouth. What is it about Callie that makes me speak without thinking? I should have practice in this based on how many times I have to keep my mouth shut around Pierce. Clearly, she brings all my walls down...and good sense.

I grab Alice's bed and a couple of toys. Callie didn't specify which ones so who knows if these are ones the pup actually likes. I hurry out to the truck and place the items in the backseat before turning the truck on. It's freezing out here and they shouldn't have to get into a cold truck. Luckily it hasn't cooled down too much.

Logistics of how this is going to work run through my head as I make my way back inside. When is the last time I changed the sheets in the guest room? Miles stayed here on New Year's and I changed them after he left. At least there will be clean bedding for them.

Callie is in the living room when I enter. Her suitcase is planted beside her. The frantic look on her face softens as soon as she sees me. Did she think I bailed on her? I'm not an asshole. At least, not all the time.

"Wow. It didn't take you long." Honestly, if it were my baby sister, she'd still be packing. Even if it's only for a few days. It's one of the reasons I hate going on vacations with her. She takes forever to do anything.

"Eh, I'm low maintenance." She shrugs her shoulders. "Some yoga pants, sweaters, and fuzzy socks are pretty much all I need. Well, undergarments, too." Her cheeks are bright pink as soon as she adds that last tidbit.

Callie blushing might be new favorite thing. I'll have to think of ways to make her do it more often.

Alexandra grunts as she pulls two suitcases behind her with a duffel bag slung over her shoulder. "A little help, please."

Both of us move toward her, reaching for the same suitcase handle, our hands brush against one another. "I've got it." My words are soft, and it takes her a moment to pull her hand away.

She takes a full step back when her daughter starts giggling. I will never understand teenagers.

Callie studies her daughter while I pull one suitcase, then the other, to my side. "You know we're only going to be at Peter's for a couple of days max, right?"

Great, she's in mom mode now. I know the sound of that tone anywhere. It's one I got from my mom frequently.

"Oh," Alexandra waves her hand in front of her

dismissing her mom's question. "This isn't all clothes. I'm assuming there's no TV so I loaded one of the suitcases with books. I have to do something to fill up the time."

That explains the weight of the last one I pulled over to me. How many books does she think she can read in a few days? Actually, never mind. Anything that brings her joy. If that's spending the cold days cuddled up reading, who am I to judge?

"You have a point." Callie agrees. She rushes over to the side of the couch and grabs something. When she comes back there's a ball of yarn in her hand. "I've been meaning to start working on a project. This feels like a good time to handle that task."

"Not to butt in on your hobby talk, but it's starting to get cold in here." I feel like a jerk for breaking the banter, but at the same time, I can see my breath and we're inside.

"Right." Callie nods and glances over at her daughter. "Since you're no longer carrying anything besides the duffle, grab Alice's leash and bring her out. We'll get loaded while you lock up."

"Fine." Alexandra rolls her eyes and moves toward the hallway.

Callie doesn't realize how lucky she is. I know for a fact me and my siblings would have put up a fight to do it. She probably remembers how unruly all of us could be.

"Do you need me to grab anything else?" I glance at my full hands. "I'm sure I can grab one more thing."

She's laughing so hard she snorts. I forgot she did that, and its actually kind of adorable.

"Sorry." She composes herself. "But where exactly are you going to carry anything else? My child has both of your hands full with her books."

"I'm sure I can hold something under my arm. I don't know." I shrug and feel dumb for even suggesting it.

"Thank you, Peter. I can carry my own stuff." She moves toward the door and I follow after her. "You letting us stay with you is more than we expected."

"It's not a problem." I don't close the door behind me because Alexandra will be behind me to lock up. "You know your brother will want to make improvements and insist you get a generator, right?"

Callie opens the passenger side door to put her yarn project in the seat before turning toward me. "I'm aware. He thinks he has to protect me from the world after everything, but despite me taking you up on this offer, I'm capable of taking care of things without his help."

What happened to her? And more importantly, why didn't Miles say anything to me? The question is on the tip of my tongue, but the door slams and I know I've lost my chance. Maybe she'll open up in the days ahead. It's not like she can run away from the question when we're trapped inside.

"Noted." I lift the lighter suitcase into the bed of the truck, and then the heavier one. It hits the bed with a thunk.

"Be careful with my babies." Alexandra calls as she approaches the truck. Alice is pulling ahead of her to get out of the cold. I open the back door so she can jump in and she doesn't waste time.

"They will be fine, I promise." I wait until Alexandra pulls herself into the seat. "We won't be driving fast enough for them to move around."

"Good." She grabs the handle and pulls the door closed.

"Sorry about her." Callie's cheeks are pink. I don't know if it's from cold or embarrassment.

"No worries. Her books are important to her. I can respect that. I wish there was something I was passionate about at that age."

I hold my hand out to help her into the truck. It's not lifted or anything, but Callie is on the shorter side and I remember all the times I would help her in and out of her brother's truck.

Reluctantly she grabs it and allows me to be the leverage she needs to get in. I should probably fix the handle that helps people get in.

"And you were passionate about the family business."

A nod is the only response I can give her. While it's true, that shouldn't have been the only thing that held my interest. Look where it's gotten me. Yes, we're successful and growing, but it's my entire life…and that probably isn't healthy. Which is why Piper is forcing me to focus on myself. Who knew I could let my baby sister bully me?

I hurry around the truck and hit a patch of ice. My ass hits the ground and I can hear Alexandra laughing in the backseat. The passenger side door opens. "Do you need help?"

The offer from Callie is sweet, but I can tell it's taking everything in her to not join her daughter.

"I'm good. I just need a second." That's what I get for running where I knew there could be ice. Fuck my life. Why did it have to happen in front of Callie and her daughter? Whatever cool points I earned from Alexandra have all but disappeared. She's never going to take me seriously.

Grabbing the bumper, I pull myself up. This is going to

hurt later. One of these days I'll remember I'm not as young I used to be. Today was obviously not that day.

My steps are much slower as I move to the driver side. The key is to act like I didn't just make an ass of myself. "Seatbelts." It's the first word out of my mouth as I get into the truck.

I wait until I hear two clicks before I put the truck in reverse and back down the driveway.

A quick glance back and Alexandra has headphones covering her ears. At least she's not giving me crap. Not right now, anyway.

"Are you sure you're, okay?" Callie places a hand on my arm. "I can look you over when we get to your house."

"I'm good." I shift into drive as soon as we're on the road and start the slow trek to my house. "It's not the first time I've busted my ass. At least my brothers weren't around to see it."

"They would definitely give you hell. Or, tried to get pictures while you were down. Especially Parker."

"You're not wrong there." My baby brother is really annoying and would probably blast it on social media. "Thanks for the concern, though."

"It's been forever since I've been down this road." Callie is staring out the window at the snow-covered pastures. "Nothing here ever really changes."

Except they have. The town's slightly bigger than it was all those years ago. She's not the same as when she left. The need to figure out what went wrong burns through me. Hopefully she'll be comfortable enough to open to me again. I'm not sure what I did to cause the chasm between us, but I want to fix it.

"You'd be surprised at just how much changes." She

turns toward me, clearly not believing my words. "Okay, so some things don't change. This road specifically. But so much has. There are more people moving to our little town and I don't know how much longer we'll be able to say we are a small town. But everyone still looks out for each other."

She nods in agreement. Though I don't know which part she seems to be okay with. I'll probably never really know because she freezes me out every time I try to make headway with her.

"How far away is your house?" She's not subtle in her subject change.

"We're almost there. It normally wouldn't take this long, but…there's ice everywhere."

I wave my arm toward the windshield as if she can't see the roads and fields blanketed.

"I do hope we aren't putting you in a tough spot. We could have waited it out at home."

"You're fine. Besides, I'm sure one of my siblings would have shown up at some point just to annoy me. Piper has a really bad habit of that."

"Hmm." She doesn't say anything else. What in the hell is she thinking. I need to know because this woman is becoming a master at doing things to get under my skin. And I'm supposed to be in a confined space with her for a couple of days.

"What's that supposed to mean?"

"Nothing." She shakes her head. "I'm just surprised all of you are still as close as you've always been. I mean, y'all live on the same property. That has to be annoying."

"More than you can imagine." I pull into the drive for Starlit Fields and keep going past the house to my piece of land. "But Paula moved to a house in town years ago. And she doesn't really have anything to do with the winery. She helps from time to time, but she's busy working at the flower shop."

"Wow." Callie shakes her head as I pull up to my driveway. Almost there. Normally this drive would take a few minutes, five max, but I can feel the tires slip on the ice. "I never thought any of you would leave the family business."

"Dad told her to do what's best for her, and she is." I don't mention the part where she had to fight to get what she wanted. Or, my big sister going toe to toe with Pierce. So far only my sisters have stood up to him. Maybe I'll be the next sibling. It's easier to avoid him for now, though. I don't want any unnecessary drama in my life.

Callie doesn't say anything else, but I can see her staring at my house. I'm not sure if that's good or bad.

"We're here."

"Finally." Alexandra calls from the backseat. I wonder if she heard the entire conversation because the headphones are still over her ears.

"Let me show y'all inside and I'll come back to get your luggage." Spending this much time with Callie on my own is awkward. How the hell am I going to spend the next couple of days with her?

ten

· · ·

callie

I SHOULDN'T HAVE AGREED to stay with him. This is asking too much. Even though he helped us unpack, I haven't spent time alone with him in years. Hell, he's part of the reason I left.

"We can get our things." The fight to do things on my own continues. He doesn't know that I've had to do it all for a long time, even before my marriage was over. It's a reflex. For whatever reason, I can't let anyone help me.

"Callie, it's freezing out here." He points at the sweatshirt I'm wearing. "And you aren't exactly dressed for this weather."

He has a point.

"Fine. We'll go inside." I point at the bed Alice is currently lying on in the backseat. "But I'm at least taking the bed so she doesn't try to claim your furniture."

"Okay." Wow, no argument from him. Maybe this won't be so bad after all.

"Lexi, can you lead Alice inside."

"Yes." The headphones are still on her head, and it looks like I'll need to have another talk with her about listening into conversations. She used to do it all the time when I was with her dad.

We all open the doors at the same time. Lexi hops out of the backseat and our pup follows after her before running ahead and pulling her toward the back of the house. My poor kid is slipping on bits of ice and I hope she doesn't fall.

"I guess she remembers the way." I lean over the seat and grab her bed before getting out.

"Most likely. I'm just glad I found her that night. Things could have turned out really bad."

He's not lying. I've seen people who've posted about their missing dog and they never found them. Or worse, they did and it wasn't a happy ending. I don't know what we would have done if Peter hadn't found her.

"Thank you, again, for that."

"It's no problem. Anyone would have done the same thing."

Not likely. It's cute that he still believes the best in everyone, though. I wonder how that works out for him in the family business. I know you can't be gullible when you're making those types of decisions. Though I'm not sure what he does exactly. I guess I'll find out more while we're here.

He walks beside me as we approach the back door. "I want you and Alexandra to make yourselves at home. My house is your house while you're here."

"Thank you. I really appreciate it." I wait for him to

open the door, Lexi and Alice stand off to the side. "My brother probably does, too."

He just turns the knob. What in the world? He doesn't even lock it. I remember growing up like that as kids, but I lock the door even when I'm home most days. He has a level of trust I clearly don't.

"Aren't you scared of getting robbed?" Lexi asks as she takes a step inside, Alice trailing behind her.

"Not really." Peter shrugs, waiting for me to go in. "If I lived in town, maybe. But I'm toward the back of the property. They would have to go by a few of my siblings' house before they made it to me."

"Who's to say they wouldn't?"

My child. She would argue with a wall if I let her.

"Most people aren't like that around here." He follows after me and scoots by to lead us out of the mudroom. We have no choice but to follow since there isn't any power. "On top of that, Pierce has cameras throughout the property. If someone did decide to break in, it would be easy to find them. Especially in a town this small."

"You've got a point." Lexi concedes. "How is your house so warm without electricity?"

As we get closer to what I assume is the living room, there's an orange glow coming from the far wall.

"Because, I made sure I had a fireplace when I built the house." He moves to a stack of wood and adds more to the fire. "Living way out here, we deal with more power outages than most when a big storm comes through."

"Is that something we have to look forward to?" I set Alice's bed in an open space beside the sofa.

"Most likely, but we haven't really had any bad storms until recently."

"So, this isn't a first time occurrence in the past year?"

"A rain storm came through in the Fall and the winds tore some pieces off the roof at the winery. Plus, no power for about a day. This is different, though. I think a lot of people are feeling the effects of this ice storm we had."

Lexi sits on the sofa and unclips the leash from Alice's collar. "They are. It seems like most of the state aside from a few areas."

"How do you know that?" I ask her.

"Social media." She rolls her eyes as if I should know that.

"I didn't realize it was that widespread," Peter says before motioning for me to take a seat. "Social media isn't really my thing."

"Mine either." I collapse next to Lexi. I have the one platform, but rarely get on it. There's too much gossip, and people say hurtful shit when they're behind a screen. I'm glad it wasn't around when I was a kid. High school would have been so much worse.

"Y'all stay put. I'll get your things and then I'll show you where your rooms are."

"Sounds good." I wait to hear the back door close before turning toward my daughter. "You really need to stop using your headphones as a method to eavesdrop."

"I wasn't." She holds her hands up, but the smirk tells me she's lying.

"Alexandra, I'm not playing. Peter is doing a nice thing by letting us stay with him." When she doesn't say anything, I continue. "I could tell him we can rough it out at our house. Then you'll have to leave the warmth and wear ten layers of clothes."

"Fine." She pouts. "I'll stop listening in on conversations. But it's cool hearing about your life here when you were a kid. You never talk about it."

There's a reason for that. I was around her age when girls in my class started talking about me. Mostly because I was always with Miles and Peter. The entire school knew I had a crush on him. It's a wonder he didn't. It's not like there wasn't a ton of gossip and rumors. There wasn't nothing else to do here aside from being in people's business and going to field parties.

"There isn't much to tell."

"Okay."

Thank God she's letting it go. At least, for now. I don't want to tell her the way I am now is a far cry to how I was in high school. The last thing I want her to think is her mom was a pushover who didn't stand up for herself.

She turns toward the back of the sofa to look out the window. "You have to admit it's pretty outside. Even if it's mostly ice. This is what I want it to look like at Christmas."

"You know as well as I do how unlikely that is." A girl can hope, though.

There are muffled thuds coming from the back of the house before I can hear the roar of the generator. Peter must be back with our luggage.

"I'll go help him." Lexi stands and heads toward the hallway. "It's my fault there's so much."

Even though she listens in on conversations, she really is a good kid. Always the first to offer help, even when it comes to me. I'm not if it's because she thinks I can't take care of myself or because she genuinely wants to help. Either way I'm not questioning it. It's enough that she's kind. I only hope it doesn't bite her in the ass the same way it did me.

Lexi comes back before Peter does. Her suitcases rolling along beside her. Alice lifts her head to see who it is and lies back down. She's perfectly content napping by the fire.

"Where's Peter?"

"He'll be back in a few minutes. He said something about checking the fuel level in the generator."

"Maybe I should go help him."

Lexi shakes her head at me. "Mom, he has it. If he needed the help he'd ask."

No, he wouldn't. He does things for everyone else, but never himself. He's been that way since we were kids. Always willing to give a helping hand even when those he helps eventually screw him over. Except for his family and Miles. Even I did when I ran off without a word. I knew it would hurt him, but I didn't care.

There's no time to think about that now. It's best not to bring up the past. I only hope he does the same. The last thing I want to do is tell him why I left. Or, why things ended with my ex-husband.

Finally, I hear heavy steps in the hallway along with wheels rolling across the floor.

"Is it warm enough in here for you?" He asks as soon as he comes into the room.

"It's perfect." Lexi smiles up at him. "It's a good thing I brought a book light with me. I'll be sitting right there by the fire for the foreseeable future."

"That sounds like a good plan." Peter laughs. "Maybe you'll get through all these books you brought with you."

"Maybe." She glances toward the other hallway. "So which room is ours? My bags take up a lot of space in here."

He grabs a flashlight off the end table and turns it on. "If you'll follow me."

I stand and grab one of Lexi's suitcases. There's no way she can pull both of them down the narrow hall. Plus, I feel useless sitting here when I could be doing something.

He passes by two doors before stopping at the last one on the left. He pushes the door open and peeks in before allowing us to pass him. From the beam of light, the room looks tidy and also small. I think Lexi's room is bigger than this. He probably doesn't have many guests, though.

He studies the space Lexi has taken up with her suitcases and looks at the bed. It's a full size, and I'm not sure how both of us are going to sleep on it. Not because we don't fit, but because my sweet child sleeps all over the place.

"Actually, Lexi, I think you'll get this room all to yourself." He says before turning on the small propane heater. "If it gets too warm in here, let me know and I'll adjust it."

"Sweet." She digs through her bag for the reading light and pulls out a book before flopping onto the bed. "Y'all may never see me again!"

"Where am I going to sleep?"

"Follow me." He grabs my bag from my shoulder and I do as I'm told. It's not far. This house isn't that big, and there are only two hallways. One that leads to the mudroom and the back door. And this one. One of the doors we passed must be his room.

"Peter, I can't take your bed." I need to voice the argument before we even get to his room. I know him well enough to know that's exactly where he intends for me to sleep.

"Yes, you can." He turns the knob on the second door we walked by and pushes the door open.

There's a battery-operated lantern on the dresser. Not that it's needed because of course he has another fireplace. The gentle orange glow fills the space and I feel bad Lexi won't get to enjoy the aesthetic.

Wait, what am I talking about? I already said I wasn't sleeping in here. It's too personal. We didn't enter each other's spaces when we were younger, why would I start doing that now.

"Where are you going to sleep if I'm in here?" It's the only thing I can think to ask. The one rebuttal that might make him realize this is ridiculous.

"The sofa."

"You don't fit on it." As if he needs me to tell him that bit of info. I'm sure he knows. Though, they are bigger than normal sized sofas. Well, the one facing the window is.

"I. Will. Be. Fine." He won't back down.

Ugh, why is he so freaking stubborn?

"Fine. But if it's okay with you, I'll hang out with you in the living room." Another bad idea. I'm supposed to be keeping the distance between us, not spending more time with my childhood crush.

"You don't have to, you know that right?" He leans his head to the side studying me. Waiting on a response.

"I know." Believe it or not, I don't want to be locked away in a room, no matter how cozy it feels. Besides, once Lexi explores the house a bit, she'll be sitting in here by the fire while she reads.

"Then why?" His eyes don't leave mine. "You've made it pretty clear you don't want me to help you with anything. Now you want to spend time with me voluntarily."

That's the million-dollar question. I can't really explain it without letting him know about the crush I harbored as a kid. Or the fact I've thought about him more than I should throughout the years, which is the main reason I didn't let him follow me on social media.

"Because I don't want to be alone. It's too quiet." It's an honest answer. More than I wanted to be.

His only response is a nod before walking out of the room. What that hell is up with that?

eleven

. . .

peter

I DON'T UNDERSTAND this woman. She's always hot and cold with me. How am I supposed to know where I stand with her? One minute she refuses my help, the next she wants to hang out with me. She makes zero sense.

The only thing I can think to do is go to the kitchen and cook. Unlike her, I don't mind being alone. It's being around people that makes me nervous. Being around her…I can't even think straight.

Every word she says throws me off kilter. She probably doesn't know she has this effect on me. The feeling was there when we were kids, if only a small acknowledgement, but being near her now is a whole different story.

Opening the fridge, I pull out the meat to make chili before setting it on the counter. Thank goodness for my generator, or all the food would have spoiled. One of these days I'm going to look into a generator for the whole house.

Hopefully they aren't picky. Chili is my comfort food when it's cold, even if I did just have it with my sister. Besides, it's not like I was planning on having company for dinner. If either of them object, I'm sure I can find something for them to eat.

Now, I only need the pot, a skillet, and the seasonings. I'm glad I paid attention when Mom was showing us how to make it. Nobody else in my family can do it the way she does.

"Are you okay?" Callie's voice scares me and I drop the pot on my foot.

"Shit." I don't mean to yell it, but it hit my foot and I'm not wearing my work boots.

"Oh my God, I'm so sorry." Callie bends down to get the pot and places it on the counter. "Do you need me to get you anything? Hopefully it doesn't bruise your foot or anything."

"I'll be fine." It's not a lie. The number of ways I've hurt myself working at the winery over the years is wild. Mostly because I refused help from anyone else. Huh, maybe Callie and I do have something in common as adults.

"Would you stop being a baby and let me look at your foot?"

"You can't see much in here."

She grabs my hand and pulls me into the living room, pushing me onto the couch. Damn, she knows how to manhandle me. It shouldn't be attractive, but it is.

"Now, let me take a look."

"I didn't know you were a nurse."

She glares at me when I laugh.

"I'm not, but you learn a thing or two when you have a kid. Not everything requires a doctor's visit."

She's not lying. I don't think my parents took us to the doctor, outside of our annual exams, unless we were really sick. Mom used a bunch of homeopathic remedies on the family. I can't really blame her.

"That's a valid point."

Her finger brushes the bottom of my foot and I jerk back, almost kneeing her in the face.

"Oh my gosh, are you ticklish?" She giggles, and sounds so much like the girl I once knew before she left town and acted like she didn't care about any of us. "I can't believe I went all this time not knowing that."

"I guess it's a good thing your brother never told you." I just know she'd be at the end of the bed with a feather tickling my feet. Now, that thought wouldn't be such a horrible idea. Minus the tickling of course.

"I would have tortured you." Her grasp is firm as she holds the bottom of my foot this time, doing her best not to make me flinch. She presses the top where the pan fell, and I wince. "It's probably going to bruise, but I don't think you broke anything. Can you move your foot around?"

"Not when you're holding it."

She immediately lets go, and I wish I could pull the words back. For once she was acting like she used to. Like being around me, wasn't a big deal.

"Try it now."

I do as I'm told and move my foot around. it's tight where the pot landed, but nothing else hurts.

"Looks like I'm all good." I stand and she takes a step back. "Thank you for checking on me."

"Um, yeah, no problem." Her eyes bounce around the

room, looking everywhere but at me. "Do you need my help with dinner?"

"I don't think so." Her face falls, and I have a feeling she needs to help with something. Not because I asked for it, but because she wants to repay my kindness. Though I would do the same for anybody. Well, maybe not. She doesn't know that though. "Actually, you can chop some onions."

"I can definitely do that."

She follows me into the kitchen, and I grab an onion from the fridge. I hand it to her and she stares around my kitchen.

"Where's the cutting board?" Oh, right. She doesn't know where anything is. This is her first time here. Miles goes through my cabinets like he lives here.

"Second cabinet on the left." I say as I dump the meat into the skillet. "I forget you've never been here."

"I love your house. The whole log cabin aesthetic is definitely your style."

"Thanks."

"And it's smart that your kitchen appliances aren't electric."

It's probably one of my favorite things about my house, outside of the fireplaces. "Most of the other siblings opted for electric. Want to guess where they come if the power goes out?"

"I bet," she laughs. "I mean, I can't say much because I'm here now."

"That's different, though." I grab a spoon from the canister and stir the meat.

"How so?" Callie doesn't look up from her cutting.

"I invited you to stay with me. They show up unannounced and expect me to take care of them."

"That's weird."

"Why is that weird?" She knows how close we've always been.

"I don't know." I glance over at her and see her shrug. "It's just, I thought they might go to Pierce for that since he's the eldest sibling."

If only they would. Not that I blame them. He's not exactly the easiest person to get along with, but it'd be nice if they leaned on him at times.

"He can be an ass at the best of times. Most of us don't want to rock the boat. Especially if we don't know what kind of mood he's in."

That's usually where I come into play. Always the one to ease the tension even though everyone knows I loathe confrontation. But they've always seen me as Pierce's lapdog, and the one he relies on the most. Up until recently that's the way it was.

"I figured he'd grow out of that."

"What?" I'm lost in my thoughts and forgot what we were talking about.

"The moodiness."

"I wish. If anything, he's worse since Dad retired. I never know where any of us stand. And he's pulled some shady shit in the last year when it comes to Piper, so we've been keeping him at a distance."

"That sucks." She doesn't add anything else. I mean, what can she say? She hasn't been here in years. She doesn't know the family dynamics. Not like she used to.

"Yep. I guess that's what happens when all the power goes to your head."

"I know a few people like that." There's derision in her voice, and I want to know who put it there. It's not my place to ask, though.

"Folks really should learn to treat people how they want to be treated." I drain the grease from the pan and add the meat to the pot. I wait for her to finish chopping the onions and also add it to the pot. She moves around me and hands me the other ingredients I need without asking. "What are you doing?"

She grins and shakes her head. "I've seen your mom make chili more times than I can count. I remember what's needed."

"It's good to know you remembered something from Asheville." The words are out of my mouth before I can stop them. Her smile falters and I want to pull them back inside. It's too late for that now.

"I didn't forget anything." Even though her voice is a whisper, it's booming in the silence of the house. "I have my reasons for not coming back until now."

"Okay." It's the only thing I can say. She clearly doesn't want to talk about it, and I'm not going to push it. When the time comes for her to divulge, I'll listen. "And sorry. I didn't mean anything by it."

"It's fine." Her tone says otherwise, but again I'm not pressing the issue. "That's in the past, and I'd rather not focus on it, if that's okay with you."

She continues to help make dinner despite the fact that I've upset her. It wasn't my intention, but I can never say the right thing around her. It's like her presence makes all the ridiculous words come out. She stays quiet throughout the process of adding everything to the pot. The silence is deafening and I don't know how to interact with her like this.

A few moments later, Alexandra comes into the kitchen. "Are y'all okay in here?" She lifts her eyebrow.

"Yep, why wouldn't it be?" Callie backs away from me because clearly, we're too close.

"Well, I heard something crash and raised voices." Alexandra looks me up and down. "Did something happen?"

I should feel offended by her insinuation, but I'm not. She's being protective of her mom, and that's something I can admire. What in the world did she see and hear before they came to Asheville? Was her dad abusive toward Callie? Miles really needs to fill me in because Callie clearly isn't.

"Peter decided to drop a pot on his foot." Callie is grinning again. At least, she can laugh at my pain.

"Why would you do that?"

I glare at for Callie making it seem as if she didn't just scare the crap out of me when she walked in here.

"I didn't do it for my own good. That's for sure. Someone needs to wear a bell anytime they're coming into a room."

Alexandra looks between me and her mom and rolls her eyes. "Y'all are weird."

Seeing as it's coming from a 16 year-old, I'm going to take that as a compliment.

"So, what are we having for dinner?" She looks toward the pot sitting on the stove.

"Chili made with—"

Calli cuts me off before I can tell her that I use venison in my chili.

Instead she says, "With cornbread. One of your favorites."

I turn my focus to her and scrunch my eyebrows. I don't even know if I have all the stuff for cornbread. "What do you mean we're making cornbread?"

"The only acceptable way to eat chili is with cornbread, so we have to make it."

She's acting weird. I can't help but wonder if her daughter won't eat the chili if she knows what is used to make it. I remember the first time Piper ate it, and her reaction when we told her it was venison. It was a whole thing. The fact she watched that cartoon with deer right before probably didn't help. If only Parker would have kept his mouth shut about it. It would have saved our ears.

"Okay, let me dig through the pantry and see if I can find a box of mix." I grab one of the lights that is have hanging above the stove and move across the kitchen to the pantry. If push comes to shove, I can ask one of my siblings if they have any. Though I'm not sure how to explain why I have guests. My baby sister would read too much into it, and I'd like to avoid that at all costs.

Alexandra is whispering something to her mom and I would love to know what they are talking about, but it's not my place. I'm only here to offer them a little bit of safety and comfort with the power being out. I'm not here to get attached. Maybe repeating that over and over again will get it through my thick skull.

It's too bad Callie's making it so damn hard for me to stay away. Especially when she keeps showing up at every turn.

twelve

. . .

callie

AFTER LEXI TELLS me I should be hitting on Peter, she leaves the kitchen with a wink. Why the hell is my daughter trying to get me to go on a date with this man? There has to be something she's seeing that I don't. Oh well, I'm not going down that road. Getting settled is my top priority. Finding a date isn't even in the top ten list.

"This is all I could find." Peter hands me a small box of cornbread mix.

I hold out my hand for the light and search for the use by date. "Well, at least it's still good…barely. What do you eat with your chili if not cornbread?"

He shrugs and I swear his cheeks redden, but it's dark and it may only be shadows. "Crackers. I don't typically cook a lot of sides. It's just me. Hell, I'd be eating leftovers right now if my sister hadn't kept the whole pot I just made."

"So, you're only cooking because we're here?" I feel

bad that he's doing things he doesn't have to in order to accommodate us. He should have to do this whether we're here or not. "We could have grabbed something easy before we left."

He reaches out his hand and grasps my arms. "Callie, it's fine. Don't spiral. I have to eat anyway, so it's not a big deal." Maybe not to him, but I don't like feeling like a burden.

Conrad always made it seem like everything I did was bothersome until I just stopped doing anything he didn't want to do. I because a shell of myself and I'm still trying to find the woman buried deep inside.

"Yeah, but you wouldn't have had to go through all this." I wave the box of cornbread in front of him. "It's too much." Especially when you add in the fact he checked on us and brought us to his house.

He encircles my other arm with his free hand. "Look, Callie, I know you like to be independent and take care of yourself. You've been that way for as long as I can remember. But dammit, stop being so stubborn and let me help you."

His fingers on my skin and the command in his voice sends warmth throughout my body. This shouldn't be as attractive as it is. For fuck's sake, I make the decision to keep him firmly in the off-limits category, and he takes charge of a situation for the first time in his life.

"Fine." I roll my eyes in an attempt to hide how much of an effect, he's having on me. "But you go to the living room and let me handle the rest of dinner."

"But—" He argues, but I turn my back to him. I need to break contact and put some distance between us.

"I'm perfectly capable of stirring the chili when needed and I can find whatever ingredients I need."

"Okay, but call me if you need help." He feet shuffle along the floor, and I'm finally alone. I really need to the roads to clear sooner than later. If I spend this much time in a confined space with Peter, I don't know if I'll be able to shove aside my dormant feelings for long.

"Sure." Little does he know, I have no intention of needing his help. Not if I want to keep my emotions in check.

"I'm going to bed." Alexandra leans over to give me a hug and kiss on the cheek. How many teens are still close like that with their parents? I know for a fact I wasn't. Miles wasn't either.

"Goodnight, kiddo. I'll see you in the morning." I continue working on my crochet project. I'm not even sure what it's going to be, but it's doing its job of keeping my mind occupied.

The fire crackles beside me and this is the most peaceful I've felt in a long time. I wonder how hard it would be to add a fireplace to my house. If it's too much work, maybe I'll get one of those fake ones. I don't know, but I'm loving the ambiance.

The door to the guest bedroom clicks shut. It sounds loud in the stillness of the house. I never realized how much noise everything makes until now. I can hear Peter moving around in the restroom. He's doing his best to be as quiet as possible so he doesn't disturb us. Which is ridiculous since it's his house, but it's appreciated.

I should probably go to bed soon. Hopefully the roads are clear tomorrow and we can go home. Not that staying here has been horrible, but I like being surrounded by my own things. The perk of sleeping in Peter's room is there's also a fireplace.

There's only a couple of stitches left in the current row to make. It feels like a good stopping point. I finish the row and gather my supplies to take with me. If I can't fall asleep, I'll be able to work on it until I do.

My sock covered feet don't make a sound as I make my way to Peter's room. The glow of my phone lighting the way. I don't hear Peter in the restroom anymore, but the door is closed and the small light glows underneath. It should be safe to go in the room now.

Except I'm not, and I come to a screeching halt in the doorway. Peter is standing across the room…shirtless.

He has a shirt in his hand like he's about to put it on. All I can do is stare. He's definitely not the lean boy I remember. The muscle definition in his arms, and back, is new. It must be from whatever he does at the winery. If I had to guess, he lifts a lot of things.

The glow of the fire makes him look otherworldly. Or, I'm giving into every fantasy I had of him when I was the girl following him around. Right now, I can't really tell. This probably wasn't the best time to walk in. He joked about me wearing a bell, maybe he should as well.

At least I would have known he was out of the restroom. Seeing him like that isn't something I'm not sure I can recover from. When did I turn into someone who longs for someone like that? The last time was when I started dating my ex-husband. Which is why watching Peter is not a good thing.

I take a step backward. Waiting in the living room until he comes out sounds like a much better idea. The crochet hook slips out of the yarn. I feel the cold metal against my arm before it falls to floor. Tinking sounds before it rolls a few inches and stops.

Maybe I'll get lucky and he didn't hear it. I want to pick up the hook, but I'm scared of what I might see when I stand. Instead, I stare at the metal stick like it'll magically levitate into my hands.

I feel his eyes on me before I direct my attention to him. Peter's focus is on me. The intensity as if he can see right through me, to my very core. "Are you okay?"

"Huh?" I know his lips are moving, but I can't piece together the words he's saying.

"Callie, are you okay?" He reaches out to grab my hand and I flinch at the gesture. Not because of anything he did, of course. But I know if we connect I won't want to let go. All the years of pining for him rush to the surface, and it's taking everything in me to push it down.

"Yeah." I shake my head to clear my thoughts. "I, uh, didn't expect you to be in here. You scared me." God, I hope he can't tell how much his mere presence affects me.

"Doesn't feel so great, does it?" He smirks and that brings me back to reality. Being mocked isn't exactly my favorite thing in the world. Even worse is when it comes from him.

"Would you put a shirt on?" I nod toward his naked chest. Hopefully the disinterested sound in my voice will come off as bravado. It's only then I remember Lexi is down the hall, and I lower my voice, "please."

Instead of doing what I asked, he leans against the

wall. "You didn't seem to mind when we were younger. Hell, I spent half the summer without a shirt."

His deep voice is somehow quiet in the room. Just act like his very being doesn't affect me, easy. Except it's not.

"Yeah, well, things change. Will you put your shirt on?"

He untangles the shirt in his hands and slides it over his head. "Better?"

I don't respond. Bending down I pick up my crochet hook and gather the yarn closer to my body. He doesn't move either. Both of us are standing our ground, unwilling to give an inch.

I refuse to relent to him. Even if it is his house.

He stares at me, waiting to see what I'm going to do. When I don't move a muscle, he sighs and runs his hand through his hair. "Well, I guess you're ready for bed?"

"Yes." I pull myself up taller. There now I'm letting him know he intimidates me in the best way possible. "I am ready for bed. If you don't mind."

He rolls his eyes and pushes away from the wall before walking toward me. "Well, then, I guess I'll see you in the morning."

"I guess so."

Without another word he brushes past me and makes his way to the living room. I swear I hear a faint "Good night, Callie."

I should have just kept my mouth shut. Or, waited until he came into the living room before I got up. But no. Now I'm going to be having dreams about Peter shirtless for the rest of the night. How do I get myself into these situations?

"Mama." Lexi's voice is a loud whisper beside me.

For a second, I think I'm dreaming. I also forget where I am and it takes a few moments to register that I'm in Peter's bed.

"Mom, get up."

"Lexi?" I feel around in the bed searching for her. "Is something wrong?"

"No, Mom, nothing's wrong. I need you to get up, breakfast is ready.

"Oh, okay." I want nothing more than to go back to sleep. Dreams of how things could have played out differently last night ran on repeat. Revisiting that wouldn't be so bad.

"Come on, before it gets cold. Peter told me to wake you up because you don't like to eat cold eggs."

Wow. I can't believe he remembered that about me. Cold eggs are disgusting. After all these years, he still knows me so well.

"Fine, fine." I roll out of bed and a sharp sting of cold hits my feet as I place them on the floor. "Hey, can you reach in my bag and get me some socks?"

"Yep." She bounces off the bed and rushes over to my bag. "I'm surprised you didn't sleep with them on last night. It was cold."

"Didn't you have your heater on?"

She tosses me a pair of socks.

"Yes, but it only does so much. Plus, I was scared to keep it up high, because, you know, house fires."

"That's a good point." I slip on the thick socks and follow her out of the room.

Peter is sitting on the recliner, pulled close to the coffee table. "You look like you slept well last night."

"I did, thank you."

Lexi laughs and points at my hair.

I reach my hands up to see what they're talking about, and I'm glad I didn't look in a mirror. Mortification that my daughter let me walk out of the room like that courses through my veins. Regardless of how I feel, or don't feel, about Peter.

"You probably should have taken a brush through that." She keeps giggling like it's the funniest thing in the world.

"You could have warned me." I feel Peter's eyes on me, but I refuse to acknowledge his gaze.

She shrugs before taking a seat on the sofa and patting the spot next to her. In my defense, Peter has probably seen worse when it comes to my hair. But still, that is not something I want him seeing when we're adults. At least, not anytime soon.

What in the world am I talking about? There shouldn't be an anytime soon. There's no relationship. No Peter. Nothing. He is off limits, and I will not go down that rabbit hole again.

"So, Mom?" Lexi asks before taking a bite of her eggs. "How do you feel about snow angels?"

"Um, I don't generally. It's cold."

"Oh." Lexi looks towards the window then back at me. "How do you feel about them in practice?"

"Why do I have to make snow angels with you? Isn't that something you can do on your own?"

"Yeah, but Mom," Lexi sighs. "It's more special when you come out with me."

I should be grateful she wants to spend the time with me, and I am, but I also don't like being cold. The last thing I want to do is make snow angels in Peter's front yard.

I noticed him studying the both of us. "Well, if she won't make them with you, I will." He nods toward Lexi. I used to do them with my brothers and sisters all the time. We'd see whose angel was the biggest. My baby sister, Piper, would always get mad when hers was the smallest. She's the baby of the family and didn't realize she wasn't quite as tall as the rest of us."

"That's funny." Lexi snorts and continues eating.

I shouldn't be annoyed Peter's offering to do this with my daughter. He's giving me an out. But it makes me feel like a terrible mom for not wanting to do this small request.

"Okay, after we eat breakfast, we can bundle up, and make snow angels."

"Yes." Lexi holds her hand in the air and Peter gets her a high five.

I'm pretty sure both of them just played me. I guess they're also getting a surprise snowball fight.

thirteen

. . .

peter

AS MUCH AS I've enjoyed having Callie and her daughter here, I'll be happy when I can sleep in my bed again. This couch isn't the most comfortable when I'm hanging off the end.

My shoulders and back are tight as I throw off the blanket and stand. I twist back and forth to see if my back will hurt less, but no such luck.

My phone dings with a text message.

PARKER

I'm going to town to see if anyone has
power yet.

PETER

Okay. Why are you telling me this?

PARKER

To see if you want to ride. And to check if
the roads are clear.

He's out of his mind if he thinks I'm getting in the car with him behind the wheel. He only knows one speed... fast.

PETER

> I'm good. Let me know if the roads are good.

PARKER

Fine. I'll ask Phillip.

I feel kind of bad for not going, but it's not like I can just leave when I have people staying with me. It would be rude. Not that I can tell my brother that. Nobody knows Callie and Alexandra are with me. If I tell them, it'll be a whole thing. The last thing I want to do is give them something to gossip about.

The door to my room opens and I watch Callie cross the hall to the restroom. I figured she'd sleep in. Yesterday was a busy day with snow angels and board games. We had a good time. At least, I think we did. She wasn't glaring at me.

Now if I could get her alone to talk about the interaction in my room that first night. I tried bringing it up after Alexandra went to bed but she wouldn't acknowledge any sort of moment. I know we had one, even if she refuses to admit it.

She comes out of the restroom and into the living room. Her hair isn't all over the place. I'm guessing she brushed it before leaving the room this time. I don't know why she's so self-conscious. She didn't used to be.

"Good morning." She says before falling onto the recliner. "Is Lexi still asleep?"

"I think so?"

"You don't sound too sure about that." She laughs. I don't think I've ever loved a sound more. She's more relaxed.

As bad as it sounds, I think she needed me to come rescue her. To have someone take care of her. It might be presumptuous of me to say, but I have a feeling she didn't have a lot of that in her marriage.

"She hasn't come out of the room yet. So, I assume she's still sleeping."

"Or, she's laying in bed reading a book or watching videos."

"Why do you say that?"

"Because it's what she does every morning before school. I'm shocked she makes it to class on time with how late we leave."

"Piper was the same way. Hell, she still is. She comes into work whenever she feels like it."

Alexandra reminds me a lot of my sister. She's outspoken but not afraid to scheme to get what she wants. It's probably a good thing she doesn't have any siblings. I can envision them getting into a lot of trouble and talking their way out of it.

"And Pierce allows that?"

"He doesn't really have a choice. It's not like he knows how to do her job."

Not that he'd actually fire her, no matter how many times he's threatened it. If it wasn't for my sister we wouldn't be becoming a household name outside of Asheville.

"That's fair. So, what's on the agenda for today? I'm surprised we haven't run out of gas for the generator. Do you need to get more or anything?"

"We're good on gas." The fire is dying down and I need to add more wood. I move to the stack sitting beside the mantle. "As far as what we're doing today, I guess more of what we did yesterday. Though, you might be able to go home."

"Oh." Is that a touch of sadness in her eyes. "How do you know that?"

"I don't yet. Parker went to town to see what the situation is. He wanted me to go with him, but I said no. He's supposed to let me know about the roads."

"Are we the reason you didn't go with your brother?" Before I can say anything she continues. "We would have been fine on our own. You shouldn't be changing what you're doing because of us."

"First of all, you were only part of the reason. I was waiting for you to get up to start breakfast." The way she picks these little fights as if she's an inconvenience. "Second, my brother can't drive for shit. There's no way I was getting in the car with him if there's ice on the road."

She taps her fingers against her leg, a nervous habit she's had since we were kids, thinking over what I said. Clearly, I need to give her some time to let down her defenses.

"Fine, but we shouldn't have been part of the reasoning to begin with." She pulls the arm on the side and leans back. "We're fully capable of taking care of ourselves."

"Never said you weren't." There's a chance the comment will fuel an argument, but I'll take it.

"As long as you know." She grins and turns on her side to watch the fire.

I leave her to it and head to the kitchen. Alexandra can eat when she wakes up, or decides to leave the room. Not that I blame her, even with the heaters and fireplace it's still cold in the house. I'll be happy when we get above freezing.

Eggs would be easier to make, but I think we'll go with pancakes today. I pull out the ingredients and get to work on breakfast.

The plus side to being stuck at home because of the weather is I've eaten more home cooked meals the past few days than I have in a while. Mostly because I have people, other than myself, to feed.

It's almost pointless to cook for myself and my freezer is typically stocked with ready to eat meals. Guess it's a good thing I haven't gotten groceries yet. The freezer wouldn't kept the food good.

"Do you need any help?" Alexandra pokes her head into the kitchen.

"Good morning, Alexandra." I give her a quick wave and pour the batter onto the skillet. "I think I'm good."

"You know you can call me, Lexi, right? You don't have to say my full name, it's a mouthful."

She's not wrong. "It felt like more of a family nickname, and I didn't want to assume it was okay. I needed to earn that right."

As far as she knew, I was just someone who returned their dog. There was no guarantee I was going to be a part of their lives.

"You earned it the night you brought Alice back to us, but keeping us warm didn't hurt."

"That's good to know, Lexi." I flip two pancakes and add bacon to the frying pan. "Your mom's in the living room. I should be done in about twenty minutes."

"Sounds good." She doesn't stick around.

Even though they've only been here two days, it's going to feel weird when they leave. Aside from me and Miles yelling at video games, this is the most lived in my house has felt.

"Home, sweet home." Lexi sighs as we pull into their driveway. "Not that there's anything wrong with your house. But my uncle has killed the mattress in your guest room, and I long for my bed."

"Is it normal for her to talk about her bed like the heroes in those books she reads?" I point my thumb at her.

"She talks to food like that, too." Callie rolls her eyes. "At least she's passionate about those three things."

"Because they are priorities." Lexi pulls Alice into her lap. "And please stop talking about me as if I'm not here. I can hear you."

Okay then. We've gone from happy teen to upset teen in the span of a minute. I'll definitely have to pay attention to my actions in front of her. The last thing I want to make her feel is like a kid.

"I'm sorry, Lexi." I nod at her in my rearview mirror and a small smile lifts the corner of her mouth.

"You're forgiven." As soon as the truck is in park, she throws open the door. "Me and Alice are going to run inside."

"You need to help—." But Lexi and Alice are already almost to the door.

"It's fine Callie, I can unload." I place a hand on hers, and am relieved when she doesn't immediately pull it away.

"I know you can, but it's also about teaching her responsibility. She won't always have someone around willing to help."

Except she will. That's what our community does, we help regardless of what's happening. Callie needs to remember that.

She pulls her hand away from mine and opens the door. Her strong, I can do everything on my own persona, coming in strong.

"Why don't you take this and make sure everything is okay inside? I'll get the bags." I slide the chili toward her. "Check for water leaks and busted pipes. I'll be there in a few."

"Okay."

There's no argument or rebuttal. Thank God for miracles. I was half expecting her to gripe at me.

I wait until she's out of the truck and inside before I get out. I hope like hell they don't have any more issues. Not because I don't want to help them, but it's going to be a nightmare getting the supplies I'll need. There are bound to be quite a few people in town making a run on the same things.

I slide Callie's duffel bag over my shoulder and pullout Lexi's suitcases. I never asked her how many of the books she got through. She didn't come out of the room much except to eat and make snow angels. Or like last night when she sat curled up by her mom.

Honestly, it's sweet they have such a close bond. It reminds of my sisters with our mom. They knew no matter what Mom would be there for anything, no judgement. I have a feeling Callie is the same with her daughter. At least, from what I can tell.

I make my way to the front door. My feet slipping on the small patches of ice and trying not to bust my ass again. We don't need a play of that incident. Lexi would have time to get out her camera and record.

Before I'm even close to the door, it opens. Callie's face is filled with frustration.

"What's wrong?" I stop in my tracks. My foot slides to the right and I try to correct myself.

"The good news is we have power."

"And the bad?"

She throws her hands in the air. "There's water all over the kitchen floor."

This is what I was worried about. I should have turned off the water before we left for my house. I drop the suitcases and bag on the sidewalk and rush inside. There's a thin layer of water on the floor.

"Can you get some towels to soak up the water? I'm going to look for the water shut off."

I don't give her a chance to argue, or question, and rush back outside. The first thing is to make sure the water gets shut off. I wish I knew when it happened. She knows to leave the water running, but they could have missed a faucet.

We probably could have caught it as it happened, but she wanted to wait to come home until I had power. She figured if I did, she did, too.

Finally, I find the shut off valve and get it turned off. There's no telling if I'll be able to get someone out here to fix it soon. I imagine they are busy right now. Fixing the problem myself is out of the question. I can do minor repairs on houses, but I'm not the one who will crawl under a house. Or knows anything about plumbing for that matter.

I grab the suitcases as I walk back inside. Callie is mopping up the last of the water.

"Did you get it turned off?" She asks as she lifts the soaking towel. Droplets of water hit the floor as she tries to get it under control.

"Yes, but you can't stay here without water."

She drops the towel and it hits the floor with a thwack. So much for all the water she cleaned up.

"We've got power, we'll be fine."

Why is this woman so freaking stubborn? It's not like I'm telling her to move in with me.

"I understand that. But you won't be able to cook, go to the restroom or take a shower. It may be a few days before a plumber can get out here. I'd rather know you're comfortable."

"But what about school? And I'm supposed to start a new job." She's looking everywhere but at me because she knows it's a weak argument.

"Pack enough to get you through the middle of next week. I have a shower and y'all are welcome to stay as long as you need."

"It's unneccess—" She begins but I cut her off.

"There's no argument here, Callie. I'm helping you and Lexi, get whatever you need and let's get back to my house so I can make some calls."

"Fine." She stands and leaves the towel in the middle of the floor as she stomps toward the bedrooms.

If having her stay those few days was a bad idea, this is probably worse. For her, at least, I'm ready to get to know more about this version of her.

fourteen

. . .

callie

THIS IS RIDICULOUS. I'm sitting on Peter's sofa while he's pacing and calling every plumber he can think of. While I appreciate him helping us when we're in a bind, I hate that it's happening so frequently.

Lexi sits down beside me with a book in her hand. "You should be less grumpy. We could be at home with no water."

"I'm fine."

She snorts. "Okay. But seriously, I don't understand why you're so upset with us being here." She glances at the romance book she's reading and then back at me. "Unless it's because you like him."

Good grief. She's hitting close to the mark and she doesn't even know about the crush I had on him when we were kids.

"Yeah, as a friend. It doesn't mean I want to stay here when we just moved into our house."

"Mmhmm." She doesn't say anything else, but goes back to reading her book.

She doesn't believe me. I'm not surprised. She reads way more into situations than she should. I guess I'll have to get a handle on my reactions around Peter. Otherwise, Lexi may get the wrong idea.

Or, maybe she has the right idea. Peter seemed to take his sweet time putting a shirt on a few days ago. Even though he's put some distance between us since that whole situation, he's more attentive than anyone I've ever known.

It's frustrating that we've needed this much rescuing, but it's nice not to have to take care of everything on my own. I can't remember the last time that happened. Maybe in the beginning of my relationship with Conrad. Back then he did everything he could to let me know he would take care of me. Until he didn't. Not emotionally, financially, or faithfully.

There's no way I should have stayed with him as long as I did. I shake my head. This isn't the time to be going down memory lane, especially when it's all the bad times. Right now, I need to deal with the problems in front of me.

Out of the corner of my eye, I see Peter slide his phone into his pocket. He takes a few steps toward us and plops onto the recliner. Why do I get the impression he's about to say something I don't want to hear?

"Well, I have good news and bad news."

"Can we start with the good? I don't know if I can handle the bad news first."

He leans back and clasps his hands together. "The plumber can come out to fix your water."

"That's great."

"At the end of the week." He adds. That must be the bad news he mentioned.

"That's not so great."

He unclasps his hands and holds his arms out wide. "At least you have a place to stay. And it's free. You won't have to get a hotel room or anything."

"Yeah, but this feels like too much, Peter." I point down at the sofa I'm sitting on. "You barely fit on this thing, and now you'll have to sleep on it even longer."

He waves away my comment. "It's all good. But you may want to go by your house and get enough clothes and your car. The roads are melted enough that you should be safe."

"Of course." I don't know why I didn't suggest we bring my car back with us earlier. Probably because I was frustrated with Peter ordering us to stay at his house until the water is fixed.

"Just let me know when you want to get it." He stands and turns toward the hall. "I need to get some laundry done now that I have power. Pierce texted me while I was on the phone with the plumber and said we're opening the winery up again tomorrow."

"Oh, I didn't realize y'all opened on the weekends."

"It's actually our busiest time. We spend most of the week prepping for it."

"That makes sense." Starlit Fields has grown since we were kids. He said Piper is a lot of the reason for it, and I believe it. She's always been competitive. And looked for ways to annoy her big brothers. It's one of the few things we had in common.

"Yep. I have a feeling folks are going to be filling up the lobby after being stuck at home for a few days."

That's not a bad idea. I may have to go check out what improvements they've made over the years.

"Most likely." I'm silent for a few seconds before adding. "We can get my car after you start your laundry. Maybe we can wash some of ours, too? I know Lexi will need clothes for school."

"You don't even have to ask." He smiles. I swear it's gotten sexier with age. My cheeks heat at the thought. "Besides, the chances of you getting a machine at the laundry mat are slim to none. Everyone will be headed there to wash their clothes in bulk."

He heads to his room. When I glance over, Lexi is staring at me with a glint in her eye. I'm already doing a terrible job of keeping my interest in him from showing. Maybe I need to keep a note in my pocket to remind me that getting involved with anyone right now is a bad idea. Especially if I'm relying on them to house me while waiting on repairs.

"Who is that?" Lexi asks as we pull into driveway that goes past the main building for the winery.

A blond woman is standing next to her car and waves us down. As she steps closer to our slowing vehicle, I realize it's Piper.

"It's one of Peter's sisters." Pushing the shifter into park, I wrap my jacket around me tighter and step out of the car.

Piper studies me for a moment before she places my face. "Oh my God, Callie?"

"In the flesh." I open my arms and she rushes forward for a hug. "How have you been?"

"Oh, you know, keeping my brothers in line as usual." She takes a step back. "I didn't realize you were back in town. What are you doing here?"

Dammit, I'm going to have to tell her we're staying with her brother. "I actually just moved back with my daughter." I point to the car where Lexi is leaning forward to see our interaction.

"That's amazing. It'll be nice having you back home." She moves her head side to side. What is she doing? "But what are you doing here, specifically?"

"Right. Our pipes busted and Peter said we can stay with him until the plumber can get over to fix it. We moved into Beau's old house."

"It's about time that house sold. Beau will be happy to know it's going to a friend." She's about to head back to her car and stops. "Wait, did you say you're staying with my brother?"

"Um, yes?"

"I need to know how that happened. I didn't think the two of you were still in contact with each other."

The need to flee is rising, but I know if I don't give in to her curiosity, she won't drop it. Or worse, she'll talk to Peter directly. I imagine she's going to do that anyway. Should I send him a text warning him?

"We weren't. But my dog ran off on New Year's Eve and your brother happened to be the person who found her. He came to check on us when the weather got really bad and told us to stay with him."

She taps her lips and grins. "I guess it's a good thing he

ducked out of the party early that night. What does your brother think about you staying with Peter?"

How is that even relevant? "He's glad someone was looking out for us. He can't drop everything and run to help while working at the ranch."

"True." Piper slowly backs away and waves. "I'll catch up with you later."

I should definitely text Peter and tell him about Piper's questions. But…I'm not going to. He can be as uncomfortable as I am.

I slide back onto the driver seat and pull away from the main building. There's a big chance dinner is going to be interesting tonight.

The sky is darkening and I'm working on dinner. It's the least I can do after everything Peter has done for us.

Is it elaborate like the chili he makes? Not even close. But it's the thought that counts, right?

"Do you need help with anything, Mom?" Lexi comes into the kitchen with her phone in her hand. She's not even looking up to see where she's going. Has she gotten that acquainted with Peter's house in the short time we've been here.

"I think I've got it." The weekend will be over soon and she'll be back at school after the unintended break. "Have you checked your school email?"

"Yes, Mom." I can practically hear her roll her eyes. "They gave us a break from any assignments in case we didn't have power. Which is a good thing because we didn't."

I'm not sure the answer required so much snark, but at least she's taking care of what she needs to. "Can you take out Alice? I'm sure she wants to run off some pent-up energy."

"Mom, she's the most chill and lazy dog I've ever seen." She shoves her phone into her pocket. "Besides, she hates the cold. I'll take her out, though."

"Thank you."

Lexi's need to tell me things I already know astounds me. But the dog still has to go out. And I need some space. Not really from her, but to gather my thoughts and prepare myself for when Peter gets here. I just know he's going to be upset about Piper knowing I'm here.

I add the noodles to the boiling water and slide the garlic bread into the oven. Now, all I need to do is make the salad. This is the kind of busy work I enjoy. There's no thinking, just making sure I go through the process of the meal I'm making. It feels good to be doing something normal again, even if I'm not in my own home.

The back door opens and I hear boots hit the floor before heavy footsteps enter the kitchen.

"Why are you cooking?" Peter asks. The question borders on an accusation, like he doesn't want me in his kitchen. "You're my guest."

I add the vegetables I cut to a bowl before facing him. "I want to. It's the least I can do after the kindness you've shown us."

Little does he know that if we had stayed where we were, I can't think of a single person who would have helped us. My ex-husband did a fine job of slowly turning everyone in our area against me. It was the catalyst to us moving.

He opens his mouth as if he's about to say something, but quickly closes it. Instead, he moves toward the cabinet holding the plates and pulls out enough for the three of us. "I'll get everything out."

"Thank you. The food should be ready soon." I'm glad he isn't actually mad at me for cooking. He must know I need this bit of normalcy. Though, I don't know how.

He also hasn't said anything about Piper. There's no way he would pull out that tidbit of information in front of Lexi. Maybe I got lucky and Piper didn't say anything to him. At least that worry is off my plate.

fifteen

. . .

peter

THE LAST PLACE I want to be is at work. After dinner last night we watched some movies and hung out. Lexi didn't say much, but she wasn't on her phone so that's a plus. I'd much rather be hanging out with them today.

Tomorrow will be weird with them gone all day, especially since it's my day off. There are some things I need to take care of. And I need to check in with the plumber. Maybe he can get to their house sooner than later.

It's not that I have a problem with Callie and Lexie staying with me. But...it's harder and harder to remember Callie is my best friend's little sister. Being around her is easy, and it feels right. Even if she's doing everything in her power to keep me at arm's length. I wish I knew what I did to her to make her not want anything to do with me.

I get my workstation set up and push aside thoughts of Callie. There's no way she's interested in more than friendship with me. Right now, I have work to do, and dwelling on why Callie seems to despise me won't accomplish it. I'm sure I'll need to restock bottles in the main house. We had a steady flow of traffic yesterday, and I except the same to happen today.

The last crate ice loaded, and I set it on the dolly. The walkway still has some slippery areas where it's shaded. The last thing I want to do is carry these out by hand and fall taking all the bottles of wine with me. I'm sure Pierce would be all over my ass if I wasted product like that, even if it's not technically my fault.

I open the warehouse door to move the bottles of wine and run into Piper. "Hello, big brother."

Why does she sound like that? The grin on her face is terrifying and I don't know if I'm in trouble or if she's trying to rope me into doing something she shouldn't.

"Hey, Piper. What's up?" I send up a silent prayer she's not going to drag me into some scheme she's concocted.

"I heard you have a guest." She smiles and bats her eyes, doing everything in her power to be innocent.

How could she know that? We haven't passed anyone as we've come and gone. Half of my siblings don't even have cameras on their property.

"Oh yeah?" The need for whatever information she has outweighing telling her the truth.

"Yep." She pauses to see if I'll say anything else. I refuse to give her the satisfaction. When she realizes I'm not going to fall into her trap, she sighs. "I ran into Callie yesterday morning. I didn't realize she's been at your house since the storm started. How did that even happen?"

It was only a matter of time before someone found out.

I guess I should be happy it's Piper and not any of my other siblings. She won't be obnoxious like our brothers.

"Miles called me to check on her. She wasn't answering her phone and he couldn't leave the ranch."

"I bet he was freaking out. He's always been an overbearing big brother. I swear, it's like it runs in the water in this town."

Should I be offended by that? I think so, but I'll let it slide for now. "He was. It was kind of annoying actually." He acts like she's not a grown ass woman capable of taking care of herself. Though, I guess I'm not much better for demanding she stay at me house. "Anyway, I went over there and they didn't have power or water. I couldn't let her stay there when I have a set up that is somewhat comfortable."

"Not to mention Miles would have kicked your ass if you'd left her there." How the hell does she know my best friend so well?

"Pretty much. She fought me on it, but eventually came with me." I'm not sure how much of the story she knows, and she's not going to tell me, so I continue. "When I got power, we decided it was time for them to go home, but they had a water leak. The plumber can't get there until closer to the end of the week. I told her it was fine to stay with me in the meantime. But I'm going to call in the morning to see if that's still the timeline."

"Why? It seems like y'all have a decent routine with her staying there." I swear if she tries to act like Eric, I'm going to lose my shit.

"Because I'm sure she wants to be in her own bed again."

"Oh, so she's sleeping in your bed?" Piper waggles her

eyebrows. It never fails, she'll always be the pain in the ass little sister.

"Not with me. I'm sleeping on the couch." As much as I like having her in my house, I'll be happy when I can sprawl out on my bed again.

"I'm going to need photographic proof because there's no way you fit on that thing. At least not comfortably."

"It's not comfortable…at all." Hoping the conversation is over, I turn toward the dolly and pull it closer to me. The bottles of wine clink together at the movement.

"Maybe we should have an impromptu game night tonight. It's been forever since I've hung out with Callie."

Oh hell no. There's no way that's happening. The last thing I need is her trying to do whatever she's cooking up in her head.

"Lexi has to get ready to go back to school tomorrow."

"She's a teen. They basically roll out of bed and go to school."

I double over in laugher. The dolly the only thing keeping me upright. "I seem to remember you taking at least an hour to get ready for school. I have a feeling Lexi is the same way."

When I catch my sister's gaze, she's not amused. She can't deny it, though.

"Fine. But don't be shocked when I invite her over for the next one. It'll be nice to have more girls around. I love you, Parker, and Phillip, but it sucks being the only girl when Paula isn't there."

"We'll see." It's the only thing I can promise her. There's no telling if Callie will even talk to me after she's back home. At least, not as much as she has been. "Since you're here, can you help me take these bottles to the main house?"

"Sure." She grabs another dolly and we load that one with fewer crates. "I'm sure Parker will be relieved I'm back."

Of course she'd leave him in charge. He sells almost as much wine as she does. It must be something about their charm. It missed quite a few of us kids. Now I just have to hope she didn't say anything to any of our other siblings. I don't want them poking around in my business.

I pull my jacket around me as I make my way from the truck to the back door. After everything was done at work, I decided to bail early. Pierce asked me to stay to help with some inventory, but I told him to get one of our brothers to help him. My sister would be so proud of me for not caving to his demands. I'm sure I'll get attitude from him at some point, but right now I don't really care.

The back door squeaks as I push it open and shut it behind me. I kick off my shoes and head to the living room. It's the most likely place Callie will be. Her car is in the driveway so I know she's here.

She's curled up in the corner of the couch working on some project with yarn. I'm starting to think it's the thing that brings her peace. She looks like she doesn't have a care in the world. Too bad I'm about to burst that little bubble.

"You could have given me some warning." That sounded a lot angrier than I meant, but I hate my siblings poking around in my business. She didn't even mention running into Piper yesterday, and that's the part that stings. That she didn't think I should know.

She drops the little hook and it dangles from the yarn. "What are you talking about? Oh, and hello by the way. You're home early."

"My sister. She sneak attacked me, wanting to know why you were here." I turn toward the hallway, ready to get out of these clothes and into something more comfortable. "After she told me she talked to you."

"Oh." Her voice is soft.

She follows after me into the room. I'm already pulling off my shirt and tossing it into the hamper in the corner. Her clothes are spread out across the bed and I wonder what she's been up to.

Instead of stopping in the doorway like she did that night, she's right behind me when I turn around to grab a shirt out of my dresser.

"I didn't think it was a big deal. Especially after you didn't mention anything about it at dinner. I just assumed you talked and it wasn't that bad."

Hearing the sadness and frustration in her voice is what breaks me. Even worse, I'm the cause.

I sigh. "It's not. I just didn't like being taken by surprise." There's no reason to pick a fight over something so small. Especially when the only reason is because I can't get I her out of my head.

"Then why are you giving me crap about it?" She pokes me in the chest with each word. "I don't understand why it's a big deal if anyone in your family knows I'm staying here."

"Because they'll poke and prod until they see us

together. And as much as I want that, I know that isn't what you're looking for." I can't believe I just said that. Ugh, she needs to be out of my house before I do something wild like fall in actual love with her.

Her mouth drops open for a split second before she's crashing into me. That's unexpected, but I don't fight her as she wraps her arms around my neck. The distance between our bodies closes as the kiss deepens. Her nails dig into my skin, clinging to me to keep us from drifting apart. My arms circle her waist, pulling her toward me.

In all the years I've known her, I never expected her to kiss me. Especially not like this. Her body presses closer to mine and I stumble backward into the dresser. Something falls to the ground, but I don't care right this second.

"Mom?" Lexi's voice comes from the guest room and Callie is out of my arms before I realize what's happening.

"Shit," she mutters. She picks up my shirt and chunks it at me. "Put this on and get out of here."

My eyebrows knit in confusion as I pull the shirt over my head. "Did I do something wrong?"

How the hell did we go from making out to whatever this is? The timing isn't great, I know that. But this? This feels like I'm not good enough.

"No. Yes? I don't know." Her words rush together. "This was a mistake."

"You kissed me."

"And I shouldn't have." She groans and pushes me toward the door. "That cannot happen again."

Before I have a chance to say anything else, she closes the door on me. The lock clicks before I hear her feet shuffle away. What the fuck? I just got locked out of my room in my own house.

She may think kissing me was a mistake, but I need to know why. Maybe calling the plumber in the morning isn't as important as I thought. Figuring out what happened between Callie and me just now, has become priority number one.

sixteen

. . .

callie

WHAT THE HELL was I thinking? The last thing I needed to do was kiss a man who just tried to make me feel like shit. Even if he explained himself. Still, it wasn't fair for him to take out his frustration about his own feelings on me.

There's no telling how far we would have gone if Lexi hadn't called out. It's weird she hasn't come to say whatever is on her mind. Good, but weird. I'm not sure how I could have explained that away. Though I know for a fact she would have given me hell about it.

I walk toward the bed and climb into it. Sitting near the edge, I pull my knees to my chest. If Lexi wasn't here, there's a good chance Peter and I would have ended up here. In this exact spot. Thank goodness for small interruptions because I'm not ready for that with anyone.

Hell, the only reason I kissed him is because he said the words I've longed to hear my entire life. It's like the teenage girl in me took that as permission to take over my body. Losing control isn't something I normally do.

My phone vibrates in my pocket and scares the hell out of me. I pull it out and answer it without even looking. "Hey, Miles."

"You don't sound excited to hear from me."

"It's just been a wild few days." That's putting it mildly. "We're still at Peter's place."

"Why? I figured you'd be back at your place by now."

"We were until we noticed one of the pipes busted. The plumber can't be there until the end of this week. So, Peter offered for us to stay here until it's fixed."

"Thank goodness," he sighs. "Y'all could have stayed with me, but I doubt Lexi would have liked sharing a bed with her mom."

"Please, all the stuff she packed wouldn't even fit in your tiny cabin. She's sleeping in the guest room and Peter's been on the couch so I could have the bed."

"I bet he's loving that." He's silent for a moment. "What are y'all doing for dinner tonight? I can take off from the ranch for a bit."

"Not sure. I bought some food to make, but I don't want to overtake his kitchen."

"Then you're coming to dinner with me. Out of the Ashes closes early on Sunday, but there's a really good Mexican place in the square."

"Sounds good."

"See you then little sister." He hangs up before I can say bye. I swear he does it to get on my nerves.

Now I need to figure out what I'm going to do for the next few hours. There's no way I'm leaving this room. And it's not like Peter can come in since I locked him out. Oh my God. I locked him out of his own room. Who does that?

There's a knock on the door. I swear if I conjured Peter with only a thought of him, I'm going to die.

"Ju-just a minute." My voice is shakier than it should be.

"Mom?" Lexi's voice is muffled through the wood. "Why is the door locked?"

I scoot off the bed and hurry to the door, unlocking it. Lexi opens the door as soon as she hears the soft click.

"Sorry, I needed a few minutes to myself."

"Why? It's not like it's horrible here." She glances into the hallway before looking back at me. "Unless…you're hiding from someone."

"I'm not hiding." Does it sound believable? Absolutely not. Luckily, Lexi doesn't press me about it. But I can already see the gears turning in her brain. The sooner we're home, the better.

"What are we doing for dinner?"

"Oh yeah, you need to get ready soon. We're meeting Miles in town."

"And that has nothing to do with a certain person?"

"No." I shake my head and dig through my suitcase. If we're leaving the house, I should probably put on real clothes. Not that my brother minds, but it'll be nice to get out of yoga pants and a t-shirt. "He called a few minutes ago. Honestly, I think he's going stir crazy at the ranch and needs to get out."

"Doesn't he usually call Peter for that?"

"I'm actually not sure."

"Well, I'm going to let Peter know we're going out. He wasn't sure if you were cooking or if he was."

So, he's the one who sent her in here. He probably knew I wouldn't answer the door if it was him. At least, not yet. The mortification of my actions is still taking up brain space.

"Okay. I'm gonna get ready." I shoo her toward the door.

"Both of y'all are being weird."

"We're really not." It's a lie and both of us know it.

There's no way in hell we're going to make it through the week without Lexi thinking there's more going on than there actually is. Fake it 'til you make it, right? I can totally do that. It was my motto the last couple of years of my marriage.

"Mom and Peter are being really awkward."

Those are the first words out of my sweet daughter's mouth as soon as we get to the table Miles has saved for us.

"That's normal." Miles waves her off. "They've been that way since we were kids."

"I don't thi—" She stops mid-sentence when she notices my glare. I don't understand why she's so insistent.

She's told me multiple times it's okay for me to date. I guess she saw more of mine and her father's crumbling marriage than I thought. Kids are too perceptive, and that's probably what's she sensing between me and Peter. Too bad it's not happening. Especially not with Peter.

"What's good to eat here?" I ask as we sit down.

"Everything. I'm pretty sure I've tried every meal on the menu. Seriously, you can't go wrong."

We look over the menu as someone from the waitstaff sets down three glasses in front of us. My brother knows us well enough to order our drinks for us.

"Are you ready to order?"

"Sure. I'll have the cheese enchiladas with queso." I don't want anything too heavy. Nerves about starting my new job tomorrow are starting to set in.

"I'll have the beef fajitas with corn tortillas, please." Lexi says.

After Miles places his order, Lexi gathers up the menus and hands them over. She starts to pull out her phone before remembering the rule about no phones during dinner.

"How are things at the ranch? Did y'all have any damage or issues?" Someone has to have better luck than we have.

"No damage. A couple of the horses got out and we had to round them up. Otherwise, things are good. I think Donovan is getting ready to hire a few more people."

"Wait, that is your boss's name?" Lexi asks.

"No." I shake my head. "That's his last name. But that's what everyone called him in high school when he was on the football team."

"Ah, so it's a sports kid thing."

"Pretty much." Miles shrugs. "But if you want to work in the summer, I'm sure he'd give you something to do."

"I'm good." Lexi draws out. "Oh, there's Abby. Can I go say hi?"

"Sure." I watch her rush across the restaurant to her

friend. At least, she's settling in. "Peter was right. Lexi hit it off with Eric's daughter."

"Speaking of, how are things really going with staying at Peter's?"

"Fine, why would you ask?"

"Because you sounded stressed when I called earlier." He takes a drink of his tea and levels me with a stare. "Plus, I know about you having a crush on him when we were kids. I just want to make sure things aren't weird between the two of you."

Son of a bitch. Does Peter know about that, too? There's no way. He would have made a smartass comment about it. Wouldn't he? I honestly don't know. Even though he's the same in a lot of ways, he's grown up a lot.

"No, it's fine. I'm shocked he knows how to cook."

"Yeah, he's fed me on more than one occasion."

"Don't y'all have family meals at the ranch?" I could have sworn he told me that when he called.

"Yes, but sometimes I want to hang out with people other than who I work with. Peter knows I can't cook for shit and always feeds me when we hang out. He's a really good guy."

I know he is. He always has been. The last thing I need is my big brother solidifying it. "Yeah, yeah. He's alright."

If I protest too much, he'll know something is up. I haven't talked to Peter since I kissed him earlier. And like the chicken shit I am, I waited until he was going to the restroom to leave the house. Avoidance appears to be my superpower.

"Does Lexi get along with him?"

"Yeah. They ambushed me into making snow angels when there was still snow on the ground." I shrug my shoulders and take a drink. "She acts like she does when you're around."

"That's good to know."

What the hell is my brother playing at?

I'm about to ask but Lexi comes back to the table with a big smile on her face. "Is it okay if I go hang out with Abby after school tomorrow. Eric said they can bring me home." She pauses for a second. "Well, Peter's house."

Oh great. Now the person who everyone says is a gossip knows we're staying with Peter. I hope like hell he doesn't say anything to anyone. Most people wouldn't be surprised with how close we all were as kids, but that's beside the point. The last thing I need for the town to think is I came back to rekindle an old flame.

Miles gives me a pointed stare because he knows I want to say no so badly. But Lexi is making friends, and I don't want my feelings to get in the way.

"Yeah, that's fine."

"Yes." She throws her hand in the air and glances over at their table. "I'll be right back."

Without another word she rushing back across the restaurant. Lexi is fitting in here more than I could imagine.

"It'll be good for her." Miles says as the waiter sets our food on the table. "She'll be running around like we did at that age. Though, you should probably look into driver's education for her. She'll have you running around every-where if she joins any school clubs."

"It's on my to-do list. I think we'll do the at home learning."

"Good choice." He uses his fork to cut a piece off his

enchilada. "Now stop stressing and let her live a little. She's safe in this town."

I have zero doubts about that. But that's not why I'm stressing. There's a small feeling in my gut about Lexi's motivations to hang out with Abby. While I know she does want to spend time with her, I'm sure she's trying to make herself scarce after her comments about things being weird between me and Peter.

My kid is flourishing, and I need to give myself the chance to do the same. It's too bad I don't know how to stop being nervous and anxious about every choice I make. The last time I thought I was doing something that made me happy, I spent far too many years in a bad marriage.

seventeen

· · ·

peter

CALLIE IS SUCH A SCAREDY CAT. She left as soon as I wasn't in the living room. The only reason I knew they were going out for dinner is because Lexi told me. A part of me wanted to call Miles and see if I could join them for dinner, but I knew that would be overstepping a line. The last thing I want to do is really piss her off. I remember her anger from when we were kids. She could be vicious when she wanted to.

Now to figure out what I'm going to eat. There's no telling when they'll be home. I open the fridge door and look through the shelves. Aside from what Callie bought the other day, it's pretty bare. I guess I'll be grocery shopping tomorrow. My fridge is almost never this empty. Surely everyone else has already gone and got the groceries they need to restock after the freeze.

I grab the jelly and close the door. Now all I need is bread and peanut butter. It's the only thing I have that's quick, easy, and doesn't need to be thawed. I'm not sure the last time I had a PB&J sandwich. Childhood is what it reminds me of. Long summer days with a sandwich as a snack before heading off to the next adventure. Sometimes I wish I could go back to those times. Being an adult is hard, and confusing.

My life used to be simple. Go to work, hang out with Miles, and do whatever Pierce needed. Now...not so much. Figuring out who I am is proving to be more diffi-cult than I imagined.

I finish making my sandwich and head to the living room with my plate in hand. At least we have power again, and I can find something to watch. Turning on the TV, I scroll through the streaming services I have and randomly select one. A movie my sister was obsessed with is the first thing that pops up. Has she been using my login again? Screw it, let's see what this is about.

It's a teen movie, but I remember her mentioning it was a retelling of a book. I can't remember which one, but so far, I like it. Pierce used to give Paula crap about watching this movie on repeat. I can see why she did, though.

Honestly, I should watch more movies like this. Maybe it'll tell me all the ways I'm fucking up with Callie. I've clearly mastered acting like a jerk for no reason outside of frustration. Hopefully she isn't still mad. Too bad I won't know until her and Lexi get back.

I'm not sure how I'm going to handle it when they are able to go back home. Them being here has been nice. I don't find myself longing for work because I'm not sitting by myself.

The back door creaks as it opens. I've been so entranced with this movie I didn't hear the car pulling in, or see the headlights through the window. Maybe it's not them. There's a good chance it's one of my siblings. They wouldn't necessarily come up the driveway.

Lexi enters the living room and laughs. "I didn't peg you for the chick flick type."

"It was the first movie that came up. I've never seen it."

"Impossible. It's a classic." When I raise my eyebrows at her she shakes her head. "Just because it was before my time doesn't mean I've never seen it. I watch it with Mom all the time."

"Watch what?" Callie asks as she enters the room. As soon as she sees the TV, she sits on the recliner. "The best part is about to happen."

"Shhh." Lexi scolds her mom. "Peter's never seen this."

The "o" her mouth makes sends electricity sparking through my body. I should not be this attracted to this woman when her daughter is literally right next to her. She mimes zipping her mouth shut and throwing away the key.

I keep watching for the best part she's talking about. So far, I'm not impressed. Then the love interest is sitting on the bleachers with a microphone and starts freaking singing. Then a few seconds later the band joins in for music.

I can see why she likes this scene. There's no way it's the grand gesture because I don't think the movie is halfway through. But it's showing interest. Maybe that's what I need to do. It seems like a better idea than being pissed off because I don't know what to do with what I'm feeling. Nobody has ever gotten under my skin the way Callie does.

"You realize that's more likely to happen in a small town than city, right?"

"Why do you say that?" Callie leans back and crosses her legs.

"Because in a small town, like Asheville, everyone would be willing to help out. Especially if the person had some pull in the social hierarchy."

"Kind of like all the Summers kids and my brother." She lifts an eyebrow.

Lexi backs away from her mom, unsure of how this conversation is going to play out. "We brought you food." She sets it on the coffee table. "I'm going to my room."

It's funny she has already laid claim to it and considers it hers. She feels comfortable here and I'm glad.

"Thank you." I pick up the takeout container and grab the wrapped silverware. My stomach grumbles. The peanut butter and jelly sandwich didn't fill me up the way I'd hoped. But I turn my attention back to Callie. "What's that supposed to mean?"

"Don't act so shocked. All of you were popular in high school. I don't know about Piper and Parker since we graduated before them. But I know for a fact the rest of you were. You could have easily pulled off something for a girl you liked."

Little does she know I spent most of my time watching her. There was no way in hell I was going to do anything about it. She's Miles's little sister. Off limits doesn't even begin to explain where my teenage brain was.

"Phillip and Pierce maybe. I've never been one to make a show of how I'm feeling."

"Ain't that the truth." She grunts.

I could ask her what she means by the statement, but

I'll let it go. Mostly because I know what she means. Even though I had a certain amount of popularity because of my older siblings, I stayed in the background as much as possible. Being the center of attention never appealed to me. It still doesn't. Piper never asks me to be in any of the winery marketing because she knows how I feel.

"Were you as obsessed with this movie as Paula was?" Changing the subject feels like the best move here. At least until I know how she's feeling after what happened earlier today.

"Who do you think showed it to me?" She laughs. "Did you never wonder where I went when I disappeared for long periods of time? I would hang out with Paula and a bowl of popcorn."

I'm happy my sister included Callie in things. She didn't seem to have a ton of girlfriends when we were in school. I'm only unsure if it was by choice or because they were jerks. It's not my place to ask. Not yet, anyway.

"That actually makes sense." I take a bite of the enchiladas they brought me. The food is still lukewarm and doesn't need to be heated. "Thank you for the food. I had a peanut butter and jelly sandwich, but it wasn't as fulfilling as I thought it would be."

She laughs, loud and long. The sound gives me some reassurance she isn't still upset about earlier. "At our age, a PB&J is a snack, not a meal."

"I didn't want to make an entire meal for one person. And…I'm out of frozen dinners."

"How do you live on those? You have to eat actual food sometimes."

"I do. Why do you think I make batches of chili? It's enough to feed me for a few days. Other times I'll go hang out with one of my siblings to get food. Or, I'll go to my parents' house."

She eyes me as if I should act like an adult at my age. I do mostly, but so much food would go to waste. I don't know how to cook for one person.

"Are you excited about starting your job tomorrow?" I have to break the silence filling the room after discussing how much I don't cook. Even though I can.

"Yes?"

"You don't sound too sure about it."

"I'm nervous. Don't get me wrong, I'm grateful to have found a job so quickly, but it feels like a step backward having to rely on help from the people I grew up with."

"Technically you'll be working for people who are much older than us. Not going to lie, though, you'll probably be working with some people from high school." I take another bite. "A lot of people left, but a lot stayed here. Or, came back."

"Like me?" There's vulnerability in the question.

"Callie, coming home doesn't mean you're a failure." I set my food on the table and get off the couch to move beside her. "You went to your support system, Miles. There's absolutely nothing wrong with hat. I hope by now you know I'm here to help as well."

"It may not feel like a failure to you, but when I left, I vowed never to come back here unless it was only for a quick visit. And here I am…with an entire house and all the problems going along with it."

"Why?"

"That's not important. Besides, it's not like I can do anything about it now. I can only make the best of my situation. Thank you by the way. I'm not sure what Lexi and I would have done if you hadn't swooped in to save the day."

What is it with this woman and refusing to give me a straight answer and let me in? One day she'll open up.

"It's not a problem. I promise." I move back to the couch because I still don't know where we stand. "You'll do great on your first day. I have faith in you."

What I really want to ask her is what happened between her and her ex-husband. She won't answer, though.

"I'm glad someone does." She moves her attention back to the movie. A clear sign that the conversation is over.

We finish the movie in companionable silence, and it's better than whatever happened earlier. Once the credits roll, she stands. "I'm heading to bed. Do you need in the room before I go to sleep?"

I guess she's trying to keep us from being in the room at the same time. I can't really blame her since she locked me out of my room.

"Yeah, I need to grab my clothes for tomorrow. I don't have to work, but there are a few things I want to get done."

"Okay." She heads to the room. I guess she needs to get some things before she gets ready for bed.

I turn off the TV and follow her. I can't wait to sleep in my bed again. But as long as Callie is comfortable, that's all that matters. Hopefully, she knows I'll go through any level of discomfort to make sure she's taken care of.

She's pulling some clothes out of her suitcase as I enter the room. My feet carry me straight to my closet. I don't want to rock the boat by lingering.

Once I have my clothes for tomorrow in hand, I turn to leave.

"Peter?" Callie's voice is a whisper above the roaring fire.

"What's up?" Don't read too much into what she's about to say. I have to keep that on repeat in my head. The last thing I need to do is make a tenuous situation worse.

"I-I'm sorry about earlier." Her eyes are trained on the floor. "About the kiss. I shouldn't have done it." She's quiet for a few moments and I think she's done but now she meets my eyes. "I had a crush on you when we were kids. Hell, even into our teens. When you said you felt something toward me, my body reacted. It's like all the words I longed to hear then propelled me forward."

I knew about the crush, well, suspected anyway. It was hard not to. But I always thought maybe she lost interest, especially since she hauled ass out of town.

Setting my clothes on the bed, I take a few tentative steps toward her. Fear I'll make her run keeps me at a distance.

"You don't need to apologize. If that role belongs to anyone, it's me. I was out of line."

"True."

"Geez, you didn't have to agree so quickly." This is what I miss. We used to go at each other for hours. Right now. It feels like we've gone back in time.

She shrugs, but I can see the smile lifting the corner of her mouth. "Maybe if I'd acted the way you did, you would have noticed me all those years ago."

I reach out and slide my hand into hers, pulling her closer. "Callie, I've always noticed you."

Her mouth drops open, and I want nothing more than

to capture her lips with mine. It's not the right time, though. Not yet.

Before she has a chance to say anything, I give her hand a quick squeeze. "We can talk about it more later. Goodnight."

Turning, I grab my clothes from the bed and leave the room as fast as possible. I put the cards on the table. It's up to her if we continue as friends or more. Either way, I know neither of us getting much sleep tonight.

eighteen

. . .

callie

WHAT THE HELL JUST HAPPENED? He drops a bomb like that and says we'll talk later. I want to talk now. Well, maybe not right this second. I'm still trying to wrap my head around his confession. But this doesn't feel like a "later" conversation. It's for the best, though. We don't need to chance Lexi walking in on us talking.

I've always seen you. Those four words play on repeat as I finish getting ready for bed.

Not once did he give any indication he felt something for me when we were teenagers. I replay as many interactions as I can remember in my mind.

I can't go down this rabbit hole tonight. Tomorrow is too important. The last thing I need is to look exhausted when I show up to work. It probably wouldn't give the best impression.

Climbing into bed, I pull the covers over me, snuggling

into the warmth. I close my eyes and will my brain to turn off so I can sleep.

No dice. Over an hour later I'm staring at the ceiling, the fire is dying down, and all I can think about is the fact Peter saw me all those years ago. And did nothing about it. There's no way I'm going to be able to sleep or start my job tomorrow until I know exactly what's going on between us. I mean, technically, it is later.

I throw the comforter off me, annoyed I even have to have this conversation in the middle of the night. My fuzzy slippers are beside the bed and I slide my feet into them as I stand. I grab the throw blanket from the bottom of the bed and wrap it around myself. There's no reason to put actual clothes on right now. Not when I plan on going back to bed, and this will keep me warm enough. Hopefully, Peter is still awake. Otherwise, this will be for nothing.

The slippers make a soft shhh sound as I make my way across the room. I softly pull the door open a crack to see if there's any noise coming from the rest of the house. The light under the guest room door is off. I would never know if Lexi is actually asleep or not. She sleeps with music playing through her headphones.

There's a soft glow coming from down the hall, but no sound. The orange is from the fireplace. But it seems like the TV must be on as well. There's no sound, though.

Opening the door wider, I try to make my steps as silent as possible down the hallway to the living room. I don't want to wake him up if he's asleep. At least not right this second.

A shadowy lump is taking up space on the sofa. Peter's feet hang off the side and I feel horrible for taking his bed.

I can fit on here without a problem, but no…he has to inconvenience himself instead.

"Peter?" My voice is loud even though it's a whisper. He doesn't move. "Peter."

This was a bad idea. I turn to head back to the room, but I stop in my tracks.

"Callie? Why are you still awake?"

Instead of his voice being husky from sleep, he sounds completely normal. Maybe his thoughts are bouncing around the way mine have been all night.

"I couldn't sleep."

"Me neither." He moves until he's sitting on the sofa and pats the space beside him.

Part of me wants to take the safe option and take a seat in the recliner on the opposite side of the room. But I'll have to talk louder, and I don't want to risk waking up Lexi. This is a conversation best had in private. We could always go back to the room, except I don't trust myself with him.

"What's on your mind?" I sit down next to him, pulling the blanket tighter around myself. It's an extra barrier to keep my hands to myself.

"You."

There's no elaboration. He merely throws down the gauntlet and remains quiet. I guess it's up to me.

"Oh." Stellar comeback, Callie. You sure know how to express yourself. I can't seem to keep from making an ass in front of him. Even through teenage me was scared to make a move, she wasn't this flustered around him.

"Yep." I can see him nod in the faint glow of the TV.

"Well, it's later. We should probably talk about…well, everything." Hopefully, that opens the door for him to start the conversation. He's the one who dropped the bombshell about always noticing me and then walking out of the room.

"I meant what I said earlier. Every time you were acting different, I knew something was wrong. When girls were mean to you, I noticed."

"Why didn't you say anything back then? You knew I liked you and didn't do a damn thing about it." It would have saved me a lot of heartache. Probably would have kept me in town, too. But I wouldn't have Lexi if things had played out differently.

"I couldn't."

"You realize that's not a reason, right? I'm gonna need you to elaborate." Where did this brazen version of me come from? I've never had a problem pulling her out with other people, just never Peter.

"You were my best friend's little sister. That's a line I wasn't willing to cross." He runs a hand through his hair and leans his head back. "I'm sure Miles would have had something to say about it, too. I couldn't put all of us in a weird situation."

As if my brother wouldn't have anything to say now. I know him better than anyone, even Peter. He'll talk crap for a bit and move on. He's the most laid-back person I've ever known, aside from some of Peter's brothers.

"Do you think my brother was oblivious? He knew I had a crush on you then, but never said anything about it. Do you honestly think he wouldn't say anything now?"

I swear, we could go round and round like this.

"He would."

"So why tell me now?"

"Well, you didn't give me a chance to tell you when

you graduated. You didn't stay for the summer or anything. Just booked up to Oklahoma and never looked back." Okay, that stings. Maybe I should have stuck around longer. "But we're adults now. And you're here. You bought a house. You're staying."

This is the most sure of himself he's sounded since we reconnected on New Year's. Any other time he's tried saying something serious it's come out in a jumble of words.

"Is that why you did all this?" I wave my hand around to include his house. "So, you could take your shot with me?"

"No." The word is out of his mouth without hesitation. "I told you it's because you needed a place to stay. I'm not the type to use subversion to get what I want."

"Then I don't understand. It's not like I've been sweet to you since I've been back. And I have a kid." It feels sudden. He's not that type of person. He makes careful decisions, and doesn't put himself out there. Not like my brother does when he wants something.

He's silent for a minute, and I worry I've said something to upset him. That's not what I'm trying to do here.

"I'm not sure what Lexi has to do with anything." He leans forward again and turns until his eyes meet mine in the light from the TV. I almost wish he would turn the damn thing off. It's distracting. "But I can't get you out of my head. Not since the night I brought Alice to you. I was fine living in my little bubble, trying to keep my sister from pushing me out of my comfort zone. Then there you are. No longer the kid who used to tag along with us, but a woman. I don't know where that leaves us now that you know how I feel."

How am I supposed to respond to that? I digest every-thing he's said. He isn't saying anything. I know this took a lot for him to voice. If he's still the same, as he was when we were kids, he doesn't talk about his feelings. He does what's asked of him, and that's it.

"I can't promise you anything. Relationships aren't my top priority. Hell, it's not even in my top three. But maybe we can see where things go." His face lights up, and I have to take him down a peg. "Once I'm back home and things are a bit more settled. I can't do this when I don't have a choice but to be around you. We can be just friends until then."

"Okay."

That's it. With all the sharing he's doing tonight I figured he'd at least push back. I can't blame him, though. I didn't really give him an option. It's this way or nothing. I need to get my life here, in Asheville, figured out before I can even think about a relationship.

"I'm going to bed now." I stand and head toward the hallway. "Goodnight."

"Night." His voice is soft. Like his admissions took everything out of him.

When I get to the room, I look back before entering. He's watching me. I'm pretty sure he didn't take his eyes off me once as I left the living room. The shiver of pleasure that runs through my body at the thought shouldn't make me happy, but it does.

Peter is already gone when Lexi and I leave the house. If I didn't have to work today, I'd be sleeping in. He's not that type of person, though. I'm not sure he knows how to sit still and relax. Not that I have any room to talk. My hands always have to be busy. It's the whole reason I crochet while watching TV or doing anything that doesn't require my full focus.

"Do I have to go to school today?" Lexi whines from the passenger seat.

"You haven't been to school in like a week. Yes, you need to go. Besides, don't you have plans afterward?"

"Oh yeah." She snaps her fingers. "I almost forgot about that. We're going to have so much fun."

"What are y'all doing?"

She shrugs. "I don't know. But whatever it is, we'll have a blast."

"I'm sure you will." I pull in to the drop off line. "Have a good day at school."

When we get to the front, she doesn't immediately jump out like usual. She reaches over and gives me a side hug. "Good luck on your first day at work."

Now she hops out of the car, slamming the door behind her. She doesn't realize just how much I need it. I let out a breath and exit the school driveway. Here's to hoping today goes well. If not, I may get a tub of ice cream to eat as soon as I get to Peter's house.

nineteen

. . .

peter

LAST NIGHT WENT BETTER than expected. Even if I hadn't planned to be so honest with Callie. I needed to get it all out there, though. It was the only I could be okay with her staying here.

Now she knows where I stand, and I'm not sure where this leaves us. I know we're friends. But can we become more? As much as I want an answer, I know bugging her about it won't do anything. She's stubborn and that much hasn't changed since childhood.

Today will be all about celebrating her first day of work. Thanks to the help from Lexi, it should be fairly easy. I guess she got up after we went to bed and left a note for me on the coffee table by my phone. Her neat handwriting listed out all of Callie's favorite foods. Along with a side note that she wouldn't be home until later. Something about hanging out with Eric's kid.

If I didn't know better, I'd say Lexi was forcing me and

her mom to have some time alone. How the hell did Eric rub off on her so quickly? Unless, of course, she's always been like this. I don't know her well enough to know for certain.

The semantics don't matter. I'll have time to show Callie that I'm serious about giving us a shot. It's not all fun and games because she's staying with me. I genuinely care about her. I always have.

"What are you doing here? It's your day off." Parker's voice scares me, and I almost drop the bottle of wine in my hand.

"I was just getting some wine to celebrate with a friend tonight."

"Oh, you mean Callie?"

"How do you know?"

"Please," he scoffs. "The minute Piper found out she filled in the rest of us."

"All of you?" Pierce doesn't need to know. At least, not until I tell him.

"Not all of us." He shakes his head and bends under the cabinet to get a bag. "But us cool kids. What are you celebrating?"

"Her first day of work." I call over my shoulder while trying to decide between the two wines in my hands. I wish I knew what her favorite type is.

"That one." He points to one of our sweet wines that isn't sangria. "Then go by the bakery and get a dessert to go with it."

"How do you know all this?" It's one of the things that's always fascinated me about my youngest brother and sister. They are able to come up with solutions and pairings on the fly. This might be one of the reasons I do most of the work in the warehouse. There's no way I'd be able to remember all this.

"It's literally my job." Parker laughs and pulls the bottle out of my hand before placing it in the bag. "Who do you think comes up with the pairings our sister puts on social media?"

"Seriously?" I always assumed Piper did all of it. The two of them are a force to be reckoned with. Now if only Pierce would realize it without constantly trying to hold them back. The shame I feel only now noticing these amazing things about my siblings is daunting. I let Pierce mold my thoughts and opinions for way too long.

"Yes. It's kind of my specialty."

"Well, you're really good at it."

He leans against the counter. "So, what are you making for dinner?"

"How do you know we're not going out?"

"Because I know you, Peter. You'd much rather cook an amazing meal than go to a restaurant. It's one of your skills. Remember that if you ever decide you don't want to follow Pierce around for the rest of your life."

Okay, that hurt. It's not untrue, though.

"Fine," I grumble. "I'm making steaks, baked potatoes, and I haven't decided if I should do a vegetable or salad."

"Definitely salad." He moves away from the counter and puts the bottle I didn't pick back on the shelf. "And if you have any leftovers, bring me some."

"You wish, little brother." I grab my wallet and pull out a twenty before sliding it into the register. "Ring that up whenever you get a chance so the inventory is screwed."

"Will do. Have fun on your date tonight."

"It's not a date." I call over my shoulder as I leave the

main house and head to my truck. I wish it was, but I don't want to press my luck.

The truck is still warm when I get in. Thank goodness because it's frigid out here. I'm so ready for Spring and warmer weather after that snow and ice storm. We are not made for that type of weather.

After starting the truck, I pull my phone out of my pocket. I'm not the most romantic person, and I need my sister's help.

PETER

Do y'all sell bouquets already made?

She almost always has her phone on her. I glance at the clock. There's no way she's awake yet. I haven't even left the property today, but I needed to get out of the house before Callie woke up.

Finally, my phone vibrates in my hand.

PAULA

Yes. Why????

PETER

Because I need some flowers...

I feel like that should be self-explanatory. What is it with my siblings giving me a hard time today?

PAULA

Are they for Callie?

PETER

Jesus, you know, too. I'm going to murder Piper.

PAULA

Come by the shop. I'll hook you up.

PETER

Thank you.

At least she didn't demand details, though I'm sure she's saving that for when I stop by Whoopsie Daisy. That will be my last stop. I don't want the flowers to wilt in the car. Besides, I don't know how flowers react to cold temperatures. This isn't exactly my area of expertise.

I wish I had Lexi's number so I could ask her what her mom's favorite flower is. Miles is an option…but then there'd be questions I'm not prepared to answer. Especially since I have no idea if Callie told him about our kiss. The last thing I want is to get cussed out by my best friend.

I put the truck in gear and head to town to run my errands. Calling the plumber is next on my list. That can wait until I get to my next destination. As much as I don't want Callie to go back to her house, I'm sure she's ready to be in her own space again.

With school back in session the roads are empty. This is my favorite time to get things done. I don't have to talk to a bunch of people and can everything handled in one swoop. And let's be honest after the storm, I need to restock my fridge.

After the grocery store, I stop by Out of the Ashes. Luckily, I don't see Eric's car in the lot. It makes sense. He's probably off today if Lexi is going to hang out with his kid after school.

It's still early and the only people inside are the employees.

"Hey Peter, what can I do for you?" Angie grins as I step up to the bar.

"Do y'all have anyone delivering today?"

"We should, but if not, I can do it. What are you hungry for?"

I pull out the note Lexi left me and pick a few things from the list. "Can you deliver this to Callie around lunch time? It's her first day at her job and I want to make sure she's taken care of."

A sly grin spreads across her face, but she doesn't grill me about anything. "Sure thing." She gives me the total and asks for the address before taking my payment.

I leave her a generous tip. Not only because I need to factor in the fact, she's delivering it, but she didn't ask me a million questions about my intentions. I know her and Callie were close in high school. Angie was probably her only reliable friend. At least from what I could see on the outside looking in.

"You are a lifesaver."

"It's literally my job." She laughs, then shoos me away. "I'm sure you have more important things to do. I'll make sure she gets her food."

"Thanks. I'll see you later." I give her a quick wave before leaving the bar. One more stop and I go home and get everything ready.

Paula is standing by the door when I pull into a parking spot in front of Whoopsie Daisy. The drive took only minutes since everything is pretty close to the town square.

"Finally," she says as she yanks the door open. "I thought you were heading straight here after you texted me."

"I had other errands to run."

"Whatever." She waves me off and beckons me to follow her. "These are the bouquets we have ready to go. The rest of the ladies are in the back working on more, but they won't be ready for another hour or so."

That's time I don't have. There are four arrangements on the glass counter, but only two contain roses. "Is there a difference in price?"

"Does it matter?"

"Not really." I'll spend whatever they are asking, though I'm sure my sister will try to give me some sort of discount since I'm her brother.

She follows my eyes to see which ones I'm drawn to. "So, the yellow roses pretty much represent friendship. Which is cool if that's what you're going for."

"Definitely not." While being friends is fine, and I'm okay with it, I'd much prefer for the flowers to signify more.

"That's what I hoped to hear." She grabs the roses in the middle. They are red and pink with other flowers I don't recognize sprinkled throughout. "I always wondered when someone would snag your attention enough to stop doing whatever our big brother asked."

Well, I'm about to pop her happy bubble. "She's not the reason."

"What do you mean? There isn't any other reason for you not being a workaholic, even on your day off."

Huh? There are things our baby sister doesn't tell everyone. "Piper made me make a New Year's resolution. Basically, I'm supposed to do things that make me happy and stop 'being Pierce's lap dog.' Her words, not mine."

She laughs because only Piper could bully her older

siblings into doing something. "Well, I'm glad you're listening to someone."

"Glad to know everyone thinks I only listen to Pierce." They aren't wrong, though. I've been this way for as long as I can remember. The need to prove myself to him runs deep inside me. That feeling is slowly fading. Pierce will only ever look out for himself. He proved that last summer.

"Can you blame us?" She puts the bouquets I didn't pick to the side and moves behind the counter to give me my total. "You always set yourself apart from the rest of us and only hung out with Pierce if Miles was busy."

When she puts it that way, I can see why they think that. Out of all my siblings, Paula should understand the most. She was the person Dad wanted to run the company with Pierce. She had everything lined up for her. But she decided to do her own thing. Even that was a big deal in Pierce's eyes and he basically cut her out of his life until last year. She's doing just fine, though.

I wish I had her and Piper's strength to defy our brother. They did it in different ways, but it was effective. He has a lot more respect for them. Respect I wish I had.

"Well, that changed after he kept Dad's retirement from me of all people. It's kind of nice not working all the time. Even if it's mostly because of the snow storm. I did tell him I wasn't staying late the other day to count inventory."

"Look at you growing and all that jazz." She holds out her hand for my card. "Isn't it great when you aren't trying to live up to other's expectations?"

"Yeah, it kind of is." I pull out my wallet and reach for my card. "How much is it?"

"Does it matter?"

I hand her my card. "Not really."

"So, are you planning something big to proclaim your undying love."

"Love is going a bit far. We're still only friends." When she hands me the card, I shove it back in my wallet. "It's nothing big. Today was her first day at her job. I'm making a steak dinner, and I'm sending her lunch to the office. Angie's delivering it."

She nods and I know I have her approval. "Nice job. I didn't know you knew how to be romantic."

"I watched that movie you were obsessed with when we were kids."

"Which one, there were a lot."

"The one with guy singing on the football field."

"So, you took notes. Good." She wraps the flowers in butcher paper. "Do you own a vase for these?"

Nope. I've never been one to put flowers out to brighten the space. I'm usually only home long enough to shower and go to bed. "Can you grab one for me?" I pull my card out again. This thing is getting a workout today.

"I got you." She pushes my hand away after grabbing a simple vase from the shelf behind her. "Good luck tonight. If she doesn't know how you feel about her after this, I don't know that she'll ever get it."

"Thanks. Have fun working today." I shove my wallet in my back pocket and grab my items. "See you at the next game night."

Now to get home and get everything ready. I need to clean and prep dinner. Tonight, I'm putting everything on the line.

twenty

. . .

callie

DATA ENTRY IS MORE boring than I remember. Actually, scratch that, I remember hating it when I first entered the work force. I'm kicking myself for choosing the easiest degree path after I met Conrad instead of going after what I wanted. There were so many mistakes made in my youth. I don't regret any of them. Without those experiences I wouldn't have Alexandra even if it hurt going through them.

I just never thought I'd be working at the local accounting firm. Anything the accountants need I get. I've also been answering the phone. It rings nonstop and it didn't take me long to realize it's because we're in the midst of tax season. No wonder I was offered a job so quickly. As much as I don't like this type of work, I hope they'll keep me on after the busy season.

The door opens and Angie walks in with a bag in her hand. I guess my boss ordered lunch for himself. In a few minutes I can push the calls to voicemail and take my own lunch. My sandwich seems less appealing after the day I've had.

"Hi Angie. What are you doing here?"

She stops at my desk and sets the bag in front of me. "I come bearing gifts. How's your first day going?"

"It's going," I mutter. "I didn't order anything, though."

"Peter did." Angie shrugs but I don't miss the sly smile she shoots my way. "He wanted to make sure you had a good lunch on your first day."

My jaw drops. This man surprises me every day. "I can't accept this. Or, at least let me pay for it."

"No need. It's already taken care of." She grabs a chair from against the wall and pulls it to the desk. "While I'm here, can you schedule me in for an appointment. I need to bring my tax documents before I forget."

"Sure. I have a few minutes before I clock out for lunch. Is there a certain time of day that works better for you?"

"Nope. I'm wide open. Perks of being the boss. I can do the business things whenever I want and I know the bar is in good hands."

I put her name in for the first appointment I find. "Here you go. If you need to change to a different date, just let me know. And thank you for bringing this." I point at the food after giving her an appointment card. The firm should look at using digital communications. Maybe I'll bring that up after I've been here for a while.

"You should thank Peter." She stands and gives me a hug over the desk. "Plus, he's a really good tipper."

That's not shocking. He seems like the type that would

give generous tips. I mean, he's been letting me stay at his house for over a week.

"I'll do that." I give her a quick wave as she leaves the building. Thank him over text seems like the better option. If I do it in person, I'm likely to get flustered and nobody wants to see that happen.

CALLIE:

Thank you for lunch. I really appreciate it.

He's probably busy and won't text me back for a while. I open the bag and pull out the boxes. How much did he order? Before I open the boxes, I get up and knock on my boss's door.

"Come in," Mrs. Hernandez calls.

I push the door open and step inside. "Is it okay if I take my lunch now? The phones seem to have stopped ringing for the time being."

"Absolutely." She smiles. "You can eat at your desk or in the break room. Whatever is more comfortable for you."

I completely forgot about the break room. It's not big at all. There's a small table with three chairs around it. But if I'm the one in there, I should have room to spread out all the boxes.

"Thank you." The door closes with a soft snick behind me. I put the food back into the bag, grab my phone and water bottle, and head into the small room. Normally I'd be fine eating at my desk, but the impulse to answer the phone if it rings would be too strong.

After laying all the boxes out, I open the lid to each one. There are potato wedges, wings, a small salad, fried pickles, and a small container of ranch dressing. The serving sizes are huge, and I don' know how he thinks I'm going to eat all this. Plus, I'm not sure how he knew what to get me. All of these are my favorites.

My phone dings and my heart beats faster. Peter's name flashes on the screen.

PETER

You're welcome. Hopefully you enjoy.

CALLIE

Of course I will. It's all my faves. How did you know?

PETER

I may have had some help.

There's only one explanation...Lexi. If I had any doubts about her orchestrating time alone with him, they are gone now.

CALLIE

My child is resourceful when she wants to be.

PETER

It worked out in my favor. What time do you get off?

CALLIE

5. Why? What's up?

PETER

No reason. But try not to avoid coming home.

He said home. Not his place...home. As if that's something that could be considered for me, too. It was probably just a slip of the tongue. My entire body warms at the thought.

CALLIE

Why?

PETER

You'll find out when you get here.

CALLIE

Okay.

PETER

For once, you're not arguing.

CALLIE

I can change that.

PETER

No, I'm good with agreement.

CALLIE

I'll see you when I get off.

He's up to something. I want to know, but at the same time, the anticipation of a surprise is enough to keep me going for the rest of the day. All I know is he's making it difficult for me not to want something more than friendship with him.

Peter's truck is parked in a spot further away from the house than it has been. I'm assuming it's because he wants me to park closer. I can see the light from the fire through the window, but no glow from the TV. Whatever he has up his sleeve doesn't seem to be watching movies. Now, I'm really curious about what he has planned. I'm not sure anything can top surprise lunch.

I grab my purse and coat out of the passenger seat before turning off the car. Putting the coat on before getting out of the car is probably smart, but the distance between me and the house isn't big. I turn off the car, open the door before shutting it behind me and sprint to the door. Thank God it's unlocked.

The mudroom light is on, but it's dark beyond it. The house smells divine, and I'm guessing he cooked dinner. Which isn't shocking except when we got here last week, his refrigerator was stocked with frozen meals and lunch meat. Maybe us being here gives him a reason to put his skills to work.

I set my purse and coat on the lone chair of the small dinette in the kitchen before moving to the soft glow in the living room. My mouth drops open.

There are candles on the coffee table and two plates sitting across from each other. I honestly thought the glow was only from the fireplace. Peter is placing a large throw pillow on both sides of the table. I'm assuming so it's so our butts don't hurt after sitting on the floor for so long, and the floor is probably cold.

"What's this?" My voice is barely above a whisper, but the room is so quiet it sounds loud.

Peter turns toward me and grabs something off the table while running a hand through his hair. "Celebrating your first successful day at work?"

It's adorable seeing him unsure of himself. Even though he never made himself the center of attention like my brother did, he moved with confidence. Besides our reintroduction, this is the first time I've seen him waver.

"I thought that's what lunch was for?" This man truly surprises me at every turn. From allowing us to stay with him while my house is out of commission to everything he's done today.

"No." He shakes his head. "That was to make sure you had food. It's not like I have a lot of options for you to take here."

"I had a sandwich." I shrug my shoulders and wait to see what he does next.

He moves closer to me and hands me a bouquet. "I made sure the fridge is stocked with things you like. And these are for you."

I take the flowers and immediately lift them to smell. I love roses. I love even more that they aren't yellow. He's serious about what he said last night.

"Thank you. They're beautiful." It's hard to see the full arrangement with only the fire lighting the room, but I know he wouldn't give me anything but the best.

"Come sit down. We should eat before the food gets cold." He leads me to one of the throw pillows and helps me until I'm situated.

I watch him leave the room toward the kitchen. Setting the flowers on the recline behind me, I study the rest of the table set up. Two wine glasses sit on either side of the table. Tapered candles provide more light in the area. There's a bottle of wine chilling in a bucket at the end of the table. Napkins and silverware are set to the side. The only thing missing is the food. I'm in awe of the attention to detail Peter has put into dinner.

He comes back in with a plate in each hand. He sets one in front of me and the other where he'll be sitting. I watch as he uses the sofa to help him sit on the pillow on his side.

"Sorry it's not at an actual table. I never needed one… until now."

"It's okay. I didn't expect you to do anything differently to appease us. This smells wonderful." I glance down at the plate. There's steak, roasted asparagus, and a baked potato. He really went all out.

"Hopefully, you think it tastes just as good." He picks up a fork and knife before cutting into his steak.

I take that as my cue to do the same. I take a bite and the flavor explodes in my mouth. "This is so freaking good." A moan escapes my lips and for a split second I'm embarrassed, but I tamp that down. If he's serious about me, then he'll take me quirks and all.

The grin that overtakes his face is the cherry on top of the day. "I'm glad you like it. How was your first day?"

I tell him about my day and what it's like working for Mrs. Hernandez. There are other people there, but she's my direct boss. As soon as I'm done filling him in, he leaves the room once again. This time he comes back with two small plates. Each one holding a slice of cheesecake with raspberry sauce drizzled over it.

"Keep this up and I might force you to marry me." The words are out of my mouth before I realize what I've said. "I'm sorry. That was a joke, obviously."

"You never know what the future holds." He laughs and moves to my side of the table, sitting next to me on the cold floor. "I was serious last night about seeing where things could go for us. I know you keep saying it's not the right time. But when would be? You never know what life will throw at you. Might as well do what makes you happy."

He's putting the decision in my hands. He's not being

pushy, but he is showing me in small ways how much I mean to him. Actions speak much louder than words, and he's nailed that.

"How would that work with both of us in the same house? I don't know that I'd want us sleeping in the same bed just yet. Lexi may have been part of this whole evening by making herself scarce, but I don't want to move too quickly."

"Not much would change. Except the fact that I'd be able to be with you. I'm perfectly capable of taking things slow."

"And if I'm not?" I know myself well enough to know I don't know how to take anything slow.

"We'll go at whatever speed you want."

I've wanted to relive that kiss for days. Now's my chance to do just that.

twenty-one

. . .

peter

I DON'T EXPECT Callie to make a move, but as soon as the words are out of my mouth, her lips are on mine. I can taste the raspberry sauce on her tongue as she deepens the kiss. I'm going at her pace. I wasn't lying when I said it.

Dinner is all but forgotten as she climbs into my lap. I don't think I've made out with someone like this since I was in high school. But that's exactly how this feels right now. Like we're exploring something new and exciting.

My hands roam down her sides before gripping her hips, pulling her closer to me. She moans at the erection evident beneath my pants. The sound does nothing to quell how much I want her in this moment. It's taking everything in me to push the feeling away.

I didn't make her dinner to get in her pants. She needs to be celebrated, even with the things that seem to be inconsequential.

Callie climbs off my lap, breaking the kiss. She grabs my hand to pull me up.

"What are we doing?"

"Follow me." She has a mischievous glint in her eye. One that reminds me of when we were kids, and she was going to talk us into doing something we didn't want to do.

She leads me to my room and closes the door once we're inside. This is not how I was expecting the evening to play out. I know Eric gave me a heads up that he'd bring Lexi home around ten, maybe a little before. We have time, but I need to know this is truly what she wants.

"We don't have to do anything tonight. We probably shouldn't rush things." I can't believe those words came out of my mouth. The last thing I want her to do is regret anything between us. Or worse, treat this like a one-time thing. I don't want one night with her. I want, need, so many more.

She presses a finger against my lips to stop any more reservations I may throw at her. "Peter, do you have any idea how many times I've fantasized about this? Not just the teenage version of myself that ran away to another state when the boy she loved didn't acknowledge her existence. But also, the nights I've lain in this bed wishing you were next to me despite telling myself I couldn't have you."

I grab her hand, placing a gentle kiss on the back so I can talk. "I only want you to be sure. If we do this. It's not just one night."

Callie moves her hands to the hem of my shirt. "You don't have to worry about that. I've been fighting my feelings for you since you found our dog. I thought I had them buried deep, but all it took was one encounter and I knew I wouldn't be able to hide them for long. Now make me feel good, please."

That's all the permission I need. I let her pull my shirt off. She pushes me backward toward the bed, but I stop her. She wants me to make her feel good, and I'm going to use all the time I know we have.

I place a soft kiss on one cheek then the other. I want to show her how much she should be worshipped. I have a feeling she didn't get that from her ex-husband. She deserves to be put on a pedestal.

My hands move down her arms until I reach the bottom of her blouse, and I pull it over her head before tossing it to the other side of the room. I reach around and undo the clasps of her bra, my fingers trailing down her arms as I slip it off. She shivers at the touch.

I turn her until she's against the edge of the bed. She lies back as I undo the buttons on her pants and slide them off along with her panties. They are soaked, and I'm glad I'm not the only one who wants this.

She shrinks into herself as my gaze moves along her body. No doubt worried about what I'll think. "Don't hide. You're beautiful."

Her cheeks turn a lovely shade of pink as I lean over her. I place kisses along her jaw before capturing her lips with mine. Her arms go around my neck and my hand glides down her side, soft and slow. Her breath catches, and this time a shiver runs through my entire body.

I pull away and she whimpers. Her hands fall to the side as my lips trail down her body. She gasps as I hook her legs over my shoulders. "Is this, okay?" I don't want to do anything she isn't comfortable with.

"Yes."

I run my tongue along her clit as I slide a finger inside her. Her hand is in my hair as I pick up speed. Her body quivers beneath me and I know she's close. Her grip tightens and her thighs squeeze my shoulders. This is my new favorite flavor, which I hope I will have for the rest of my life.

Her body stills. Her legs fall off my shoulders, limp. I stand and undo the button of my jeans before sliding them down. The nightstand drawer squeaks as I pull it open to get a condom. I need to fix it, but that's a problem for another day. Right now, my focus is on Callie.

"Sorry, that was so fast." She covers her face with her hands. "It's, uh, been a while."

I roll the condom over myself and pull her hands from her face. "You never have to apologize to me. Especially about this."

"Okay." She glances around the room before her eyes meet mine. "Can I be on top?"

I'm not sure I've ever talked this much while having sex, but I want Callie to be comfortable. The fact she's asking instead of demanding the way she did when she dragged me into the room worries me. Did her ex not give her any say in the bedroom? Now isn't the time to ask.

"If that's what you want. You never need ask. Tell me what you want, and I'll gladly do it."

"Okay."

She waits for me to get on the bed before climbing over me. I sweep her hair to the side. I want to see her. I pull her down to me, kissing her so she doesn't feel so awkward. If it's been a while, she may feel out of her element. I don't want her to overthink this.

Her body loosens up, and she's grinding against me. One hand is on the headboard, and the other moves to grab my cock. She pumps it once, twice, three times before lifting and sliding over me.

"Fuck, Callie," I whisper against her lips. I feel her smile before she deepens the kiss and rides me with confidence. Damn, she feels good. Too good. There's no way in hell I'm ever going to give this up.

I slide my fingers into her hair, with one hand, gripping the strands between my fingers. For a second I worry it's the wrong thing to do, but she moans into my mouth and I know she likes it. My other hand slides to her hip. I need her to slow down. If not, I won't last much longer.

She grinds into me harder before breaking the kiss and sitting up as she tightens around me. There's no way in hell I'll be able to hold back. I move my other hand to hip and pump into her as she finds her release before I follow along after her.

Her breath is short as she bends down to lie on my chest. "That was…thank you."

"Did you just thank me for sex?" I chuckle.

"You have no idea how much I needed that." I can feel her lips turn up in a smile against my skin.

"Same." It's the only thing I can think to say. I'm too chicken shit to tell her it's been a while for me, too. Dating has been on the back burner since I work all the damn time.

"Happy to know it's not just me." She rolls to the side of the bed. "I should probably take a shower before Lexi gets home."

"Do you need help?"

She swats my chest with her hand. "If you help, I'm not sure we'll be quick."

"Fine." I pout. "I guess I'll get dressed and clean up our dinner mess."

"I'll help with the dishes as soon as I'm out."

"You don't have to do that. Tonight is supposed to be all about you."

"I want to." She leans over and gives me a quick kiss before rolling off the bed. It's nice seeing her so carefree. I don't think she's been this light-hearted since she moved back. Maybe it means she's finally feeling secure in her life. A small part of me hopes I'm helping with it.

"I'm gonna run to the restroom real quick while you get your stuff together."

"Take your time."

I'm loath to get out of my bed. I've missed it in the last week. But if I don't get up now, there's a good chance I'll fall asleep, and there's no way she'll be able to convince me to move.

I take a few minutes to dispose of the condom and clean up before going back to my room. As soon as the bathroom is free, a towel-wrapped Callie heads for it. It takes only a couple of minutes for me to throw on a pair of sweats and a t-shirt.

While Callie's in the shower, I straighten up the bed. I noticed the bed is always made as soon as she leaves the room. The bed only gets made when I have people coming over. It's never high on my priority list.

Next up are the clothes. I put my dirty clothes in the hamper in my closet and move Callie's to the small pile she has on the floor. After work tomorrow, I'll get something for her dirty clothes.

I hear the bathroom door open as I finish cleaning my room, and Callie's walking in with wet hair.

"Cute jammies." I nod at her pink pajama set covered in hearts.

"They're warm."

"Doesn't make them less cute."

"Well, if you had central air and heat, I wouldn't be so cold." She sticks her tongue out at me.

"It's never been an issue until now. I'm hardly ever home, and the fireplaces and window units are usually enough." But you bet that's going to change in the future. I want my house to be comfortable for her.

"I'm only giving you a hard time. Let's get the dishes cleaned up." She moves to the hallway, and I follow her. She stops in her tracks. "Alice, no."

I lean over to see why she's yelling at the pup. Alice is licking the plates. "Hopefully, there isn't anything on there that will make her sick."

"If only you knew the things we've walked in on her eating. She thinks she's being sneaky, but gets caught every time." Callie shakes her head and hurries to the coffee table to grab the plates.

Luckily, Alice didn't knock over the candles. I didn't think to blow them out before we left the room. I blow them out and turn on the lights. Cleanup will be easier if we can see everything.

We're finishing up the dishes when the door to the mudroom opens. "I'm home." Lexi yells louder than necessary.

"We see that." Callie laughs. "There's a slice of cheese-cake for you in the fridge."

"You do love me."

"That's all Peter. He's the one who got it for you. Did you have fun with Abby?"

"Yes!" She goes to the fridge to get her dessert, and when she turns around Callie is leaning against me with her arm around my waist.

"My plan worked." She throws a hand in the air.

"I knew there was a reason you wanted to go to a friend's house on a school night." Callie sighs.

"A girl's gotta do what a girl's gotta do. Besides, you deserve to be happy."

Maybe her being friends with Eric's kid isn't such a great idea. She'll be running around trying to play matchmaker, too. Though, I'm glad she thinks I make her mom happy. Now I need to make sure I keep it up. And figure out how to tell Miles I'm dating his little sister.

twenty-two

. . .

callie

LAST NIGHT WAS AMAZING. Peter showed me appreciation I've never experienced. Conrad did nothing like that when we were married. Hell, he didn't even do it when we first started dating.

Everything Peter did last night truly felt like princess treatment. Like I was the only person who mattered. I can't stop thinking about the way his hands felt on my body. I wasn't lying when I said I had fantasized about it for years.

"You are smiley this morning, Mom." Lexi says as she comes into my room. "I'm guessing date night was good."

"Yes. But you realize you probably shouldn't be setting your parent up with dates, right? This isn't a movie." I finish curling one last strand of hair. It's going to take a while to get used to having to get up and get ready.

"I want you to be happy." She shrugs and sets her

backpack on the floor before climbing on the bed. "If I have to make sure it happens, then I will."

I turn off my curling iron and set it on the dresser before taking a seat on the bed next to my daughter. "Are you sure you're okay with me and Peter dating? I don't want to do anything that will make you uncomfortable. You are and will always be my main priority."

She turns toward me and grabs my hands. "Mom, I mean this with all the love in my heart. Do not make dating decisions based on me. I know Dad was shitty. I heard the arguments and him coming in really late when you thought I was asleep. His side of the family has always treated you differently and made things hard on us when you got a divorce. You deserve to feel special, and be with someone who shows it."

My eyes tear up, and I pull my hands out of hers to wave away the moisture. It's too early in the morning for her to make me cry. "When did you become so wise?"

"I've always been this way." Her smile is cocky and I'm glad she's so sure of herself. "Hurry up before you're late to work. You can't make a bad impression on your second day."

Oh, how the tables have turned. It's usually her I'm dragging out of bed to get to school. "Okay. I just need to grab my shoes."

"I'll wait in the kitchen." She slides off the bed and grabs her backpack before heading out of the room. She's so grown-up. I have no clue how I'm going to handle it when she goes off to college or whatever her next adventure will be. She's right, though. I need to start living for me.

I get off the bed and grab my shoes from beside the

dresser. One last look in the mirror to make sure the wetness in my eyes didn't ruin my mascara and I'm ready for the day.

When I get to the kitchen, Lexi is staring at something on the table. "What is it?"

"He's a keeper, Mom." She points at the soft pink lunchbox sitting in the middle of the table.

There's a note attached to the box, and I pick it up to read it.

Have a great day at work. I'll see you when I get home.

There's that word again…home. It's wild how much he feels like home even though it hasn't been long since we've reconnected. A girl could get used to this.

Only ten more minutes until I get to leave work for the day. Alexandra texted me earlier saying she's getting a ride home from Joan. That is a weight off my shoulders. At least, for today. I should probably find out what time the bus runs down our road. I don't want to rely on other people to get her home all the time. I feel bad.

It's the one thing I miss about living in our old neighborhood. Lexi was able to walk to and from school. At least it looks like we already have a community here to help out when needed. The perks of living in a small town where everyone knows you.

I begin the process of shutting everything down and

clear off my desk. It doesn't take long because there's nothing of my own on it. My bright pink water cup is the only spot of color. Maybe I should ask if I can bring a couple of pictures to put on here. Something to make it my own space.

There are a few things I need to take care of first thing in the morning, and I put those sticky notes on my monitor so I don't forget. This is probably the most organized space in my life, and it brings me peace knowing I won't be a mess when I come in tomorrow.

Mrs. Hernandez comes out of her office and glances over my desk. "You can head out now. It's a good idea to take advantage of the early days while you can. There will be a couple of weeks in the coming months where I'll need you here later."

"Oh, okay." I'm not sure why I'd need to be here later than that.

"It won't be a lot of extra work. Just making sure people have everything they need for their taxes. We'll get a rush of people coming in at the last possible second to get their taxes done for the year."

"That makes sense. People love to procrastinate."

"Unfortunately. They know it happens at the same time every year, but they are shocked when the deadline approaches. But that's why they come to me. They know I'll get them done and help them out as much as I can."

I love that I have a boss who is confident in their work. Plus, she's not constantly watching over my shoulder and trusts me to do my job.

"That is something I can understand. My daughter is the queen of procrastination." I grab my purse out of the bottom drawer of my desk and sling it over my shoulder. "Have a great night."

"You too."

My steps are quick as I leave the office and head to my car. I barely have it turned on before my phone rings through my speakers.

I hit answer on my steering wheel as I put my purse in the passenger seat and secure my seatbelt.

"Hey Miles."

"How's the job going? I trust Mrs. Hernandez is treating you well." The wind is loud in the receiver and I wish he'd call me when he's done with all his responsibilities.

"It's good. The work is fairly easy and she's sweet."

"That's good." He grunts as he does something and I'm too afraid to ask what he's doing. "How are things going at Peter's? Any word from the plumber?"

Crap. Do I tell him about me and Peter now? I'm not going to tell him we had sex obviously, but does he need to know we're seeing each other? Probably. I mean he knew every detail about my marriage, there's no reason not to tell him.

"No word from the plumber. Though, I'm sure he'll call Peter." I take a deep breath and let the next words rush out of my mouth. "Peter and I are dating."

The line is quiet for a while. I know he didn't disconnect because I can hear ranch sounds. "It's about time."

Wait, what? He knew about the crush when we were kids, but I didn't expect him to be excited about this new label.

"You're not mad?"

"Why would I be? Two of my favorite people finding

happiness. It's the best thing I could hope for. But I will break his hands if he hurts you."

I can't help the laugh that bursts out as I pull out of my parking spot. "I don't think you have to worry about that."

"How long has this been going on. I just saw you two days ago."

"Since last night. He told me how he felt about me after dinner Sunday, but the way he shows up without any prompting is what won me over."

"Good. As long as he makes you happy, I'm good with it." There's a rustling sound before he speaks again. "I was actually coming by his place tonight. It's been a while since I've seen him. Hopefully, he's making something good for dinner and not feeding you frozen dinners."

"You realize I'm fully capable of making my own dinners. I've been doing it for years."

"I know, but why not let someone else take care of you for a while. You've taken care of other people for so long. It's your turn."

That's exactly what Peter has been doing…since I came back to town.

"If you say so. I'll see you later."

"Bye, sis."

I end the call and continue driving toward Peter's house. Knowing my brother isn't mad about the two of us dating eases a fear I didn't realize I had until I blurted out the words.

To my shock, Peter's truck is already in the driveway when I get there. I was under the impression that he worked late most days. At least, that's what my brother told me. It's not a bad thing, I just don't want him to change everything because we're dating or living with him for the time being.

Before I'm out of the car, Lexi runs outside in yoga pants and a hoodie. How is she not freezing? "Put on some warmer clothes. You're going to get sick."

She waves away my concern. "There's a surprise inside, but I need to cover your eyes before you go in. We need the full effect."

We? What have she and Peter done now? I'm never going to survive them if they keep teaming up on things. Though I don't think he knew Lexi orchestrated the alone time last night until she said something.

"What did the two of you do?" I don't even know why I asked the question. It's not like she's going to tell me.

"You'll see." She claps her hands together and jumps. I think it might be from a mixture of excitement and trying to warm up. "Obviously, you can keep your eyes open until we get to the door. But then, my hands go in front of them."

There's no use arguing. I hurry to the door if only to keep my child from getting sick since she isn't displaying any form common sense when it comes to outwear.

As soon as I turn the knob and take a step inside, her hands fly over my eyes. "Can you see anything?"

"Nope. But let me slide my shoes off before we move."

"Hurry." Whatever it is she wants to show me must be big because she only shows this much emotion over books and music. I slip my shoes off and wait for further instructions. "Now take small steps straight forward. Then I'll turn you in the direction you need to go."

I'm trusting she isn't going to make me fall flat on my

face. That would put a damper on their surprise. I do as she asks and stop after she turns my body to the left.

"You can open your eyes now." Peter's voice is right next to me.

Lexi lifts her hands form my eyes and I gasp. The dinette that was sitting in this space this morning is gone. In its place is a kitchen table that will fit at least six people. It makes the dining area look full. Which isn't a bad thing considering it looked lopsided with that sad little table in the middle.

"What? When? Where did the other table go?" The questions tumble out of my mouth.

Peter laughs and Lexi squeals. "Isn't it beautiful? No more eating on the floor."

I move forward and run my hands along the dark brown wood. It fits with the whole log cabin thing he has going on here. It's brand freaking new.

Peter moves beside and pulls me into a hug. "Do you like it?"

"Yes. But why? It's not like we're going to be here forever. You didn't have to change anything."

He stares down at me as if I've just asked a ridiculous question. "Because it'll be nice to eat dinner together at a table. The coffee table worked when it was just me. But I see a lot of dinners in our future. Plus, it's harder for Alice to jump up and try to eat any leftovers."

"Wait, Alice did what?" Lexi asks.

"Last night when we started cleaning up, we found Alice licking the plates on the coffee table." I shake my head remembering the sight.

"My dog would never." Lexi puts her hand over her

heart in mock outrage. "Well, I'm going to do homework. You two have fun."

She rushes out of the room and I have zero doubts she'll actually be reading a book instead of doing the homework she needs to do.

"Need help cooking dinner?" I look up at Peter.

"Sure." He leans down and captures my lips with his. I could get used to this sort of welcome. Finally, he breaks the kiss. "Now we can cook dinner."

Yeah, I'm going to miss this when we can finally go back home.

twenty-three

. . .

peter

CALLIE and I move as one throughout the kitchen. Each takes care of a task while we prepare dinner. It's almost like a dance, and I can't believe the two of us can share a space like this without bumping into each other. I don't even have this easy of a workflow with my siblings and we've worked together for literal years.

I hear a vehicle outside, and I think nothing of it. It's likely one of my brothers out on the golf cart because they're bored, or nosy. They always have to know what everyone else is up to. The old ladies in town have nothing on my siblings when it comes to gossip. Moments later, the sound stops, and there's a knock at the back door. Everyone who is supposed to be here is already here. Nobody in my family knocks. They barge in as if they own the place. I have no idea who it could be. Anyone who visits comes to the front door.

I turn toward the back of the house and see Callie

flinch before she faces me. "I may have forgotten to mention my brother said he was going to stop by. He's having Peter withdrawals."

"You know, from anyone on the outside looking in, their mind would go straight to the gutter."

"As if yours isn't." Callie's giggle sends waves of happiness through me.

I make my way to the mudroom and open the back door. Miles is in fact here. He's rubbing his hands together to stay warm. I would have thought the cold didn't bother him as much since he works in it.

"It's about time. It's freezing out here."

"I don't know why you knocked. You usually come right in."

"Yeah, but that's before you were dating my sister. I don't want to walk in on anything that'll give me nightmares."

My feet stick to the floor at his statement. Oh shit. "When did you find out?"

"Callie told me earlier. I guess she forgot to tell you." He shakes his head.

"Is that why you came over? To tell me not to hurt your sister." I don't want Callie to hear anything I'm saying in case it upsets her, so I keep my voice low.

"I had already planned on dropping by. I haven't seen you since before the storm. But the hurting my sister part, that's a given. I didn't think I'd need to voice it."

"You don't because I have no intention of hurting her."

"Good." He claps me on the shoulder. "I'm glad the two of you are finding happiness. Now, what's for dinner?"

That's my best friend. Always thinking about food.

Well, that went better than expected. I thought things might be weird, but nope. Miles handled our hand-holding and snuggling with grace. He didn't even make a face. Hopefully, my family is the same way when we show up together at a function.

"So, next month we're doing a Valentine's Day thing at the winery, would you like to be my date?"

"When did you start doing events? I don't remember y'all doing anything except bottling and selling wine." Callie scratches her head in confusion.

"Piper and Paula have made it their mission to bring the community to the winery. Offering events is what is getting them here. We used to do things with Out of the Ashes at the bar. It was a win-win situation." I grip her hand in mine. "Now, they want to do it all in house. Piper said it builds brand recognition."

"She has a point. Your little sister has always been someone who thinks out of the box."

"Yep. It caused some issues in the fall because Pierce didn't want to hand over anything to Piper. It as a whole thing. He even roped Beau into it. That caused some friction between the siblings. Since then, she hasn't really talked to Pierce. I don't blame her one bit."

She thinks over my words for a bit. "I don't either. Pierce has always been…intense. I remember one time he yelled at me when we were kids because I was playing behind one of the barrels. By his reaction, you would have thought I had committed some treasonous crime."

"That tracks. He's pissed at me right now because I'm

leaving work at the time I'm supposed to instead of staying late." I take a drink of my hot chocolate. It seemed like a great drink for this evening. I never really kept any in the house until now. I know she liked it when we were kids. And Lexi mentioned it one night during the ice storm. "It's kind of annoying. The only people he comes down hard on are me and Piper. It's like he doesn't care what anyone else does as long as he can keep his thumb on us."

"That sounds about right. I see not much has changed with him since our younger years." She snuggles closer into my side as we watch TV. I don't know what we're watching, but it's basically background noise at this point. "Any other exciting news at Starlit Fields?"

"Other than my dad retiring? Not really." I shrug. It's still business as usual in regards to everything else. "I know we'll need to hire more people soon for the weekend crowd. Most of us can handle the few hours we're open during the week, but the weekends are busier than they've ever been, thanks to Piper."

"That's good. Who knows maybe I'll apply. The extra cash couldn't hurt." She laughs as soon as she says so I know she's not serious.

"Believe me, you do not want to work under Pierce. I feel sorry for whoever we hire. Thankfully, they'll spend most of their time with Piper unless she has a tasting event. Then they'll report directly to Pierce."

"Yeah, no thanks. I love your siblings. Well, most of them. But I would butt heads with your big brother, so much."

"You're not the only one."

Callie pulls a blanket off the back of the couch and

pulls it over the both of us. "I need to figure out what time the bus runs out here. As much as I appreciate Eric and his partner, I can't rely on them to get Lexi home every day."

"Has she ever ridden a bus?"

"For school trips." She shrugs her shoulders. "But it's not like she's five. She'll figure it out."

"What time does she get out of school?"

"Almost four, I think." She shakes her head. "I really need to get on the ball with getting her a license."

"Lexi," I call. I don't know if she can hear me because she probably has her headphones on. I'm moving the blanket when the door down the hall opens, and she hurries down the hall.

"Yeah?" Why does she look guilty? It's not my job to parent her. I'm sure if anything's amiss Callie will call her out on it.

"Do you want to ride the bus after school?" The face she gives in response is the only answer I need. "I'll pick her up, then."

"You don't need to leave work early to pick her up." Callie argues.

"I won't be. I get off around three."

"What?" Callie shrieks. "Miles told me you work late all the time."

"By choice, not because I have to. It's not like I had anything better to do. Miles is always busy at the ranch and I didn't have anyone waiting at home with me."

Out of the corner of my eye, Lexi gives me a thumbs up and walks backward to her room without making a noise. I guess she thinks we have it from here.

"And what about when we can go back home? Will

you still work late?" She's waiting to see what I say, as if the answer is very important.

"No. Just because you're not at home doesn't mean I won't hurry to see you and Lexi." She doesn't realize how important she's become to me. How important both of them are. "I told you, I'm all in. Last night wasn't a fluke."

Callie breathes a sigh of relief and leans her head against the couch. "Okay."

I turn toward her and cup her face with one hand. "What the hell happened in your marriage that you even have to ask that?"

She doesn't have to tell me, I know that. But I hope like hell she opens up. I can't reassure her if I don't know what the core problem is.

"He cheated…a lot." She takes a deep breath. "Everything was fine-ish in the beginning. Even after we had Lexi. Then he'd start working late and not even come home sometimes. I put up with it for a lot longer than I should have. But Conrad, and his family, made it clear I couldn't raise a child on my own. That I couldn't make it without them. I was young and hopeful he would change every time he said he would."

"But he didn't." I don't phrase as a question because it's not. I can tell by the pain that his behavior continued.

"I changed so much about myself to make him want me. To come home to me instead of someone else, but it was useless. He was going to keep cheating and I either had to deal with it or leave. It took everything in Miles not to beat the crap out of him when he'd visit. But I wanted to keep the peace. For the past year Miles came up at least once a month to help me with lawyers and find a house down here. I needed to be with family. I couldn't take it anymore."

Now all of Miles's trips out of town make sense. I thought Colton was sending him places on ranch business. The whole time he was helping his sister get out of a shitty situation.

"First of all, it's his loss. Nobody in their right mind wouldn't want you. You're beautiful, smart, funny, and independent. I'm glad you left. But why didn't you call me to help? I would have come in a heartbeat. I thought we were better friends than that."

She laughs. But it's not because anything's funny. It's self-deprecating. "There was no way I was calling you. I left because it hurt too much to be around you and you not noticing me as anything more than Miles's little sister. It didn't help that some girls in my class gave me crap about it and called me pathetic. When I got the scholarship to a school in Oklahoma, I took it and never looked back. I couldn't let you see how horribly my life turned out."

Fuck. She's breaking my heart as much as she did when she left and broke all contact without an explanation.

"I'm sorry."

"For what?" She's genuinely confused.

"Everything. If I had asked you out back then, all of this could have been avoided. I was too worried about what Miles would think, and what it would change with my friend if things didn't work out."

"That wasn't all on you," she argues. "Besides, if things didn't play out exactly how they did, I wouldn't have Lexi. Or this chance with you."

I hold up my mug of hot chocolate and clink it to hers. "Here's to second chances."

twenty-four

. . .

callie

"I'VE GOT GOOD NEWS." Peter announces as he comes into the bedroom.

"What are you still doing here? You're always gone by the time we leave for school and work." I'm putting my shirt on and I'm certain the words are muffled. Hopefully he gets the gist of what I'm saying.

"True, but I'm going in late today." He rushes to me and wraps his arms around my waist. It feels like a bear hug the way he envelopes me. "Can I get the key to your house?"

"Why?" I catch his eyes in the mirror.

"Because the good news is the plumber called me as I was about to head out the door. He's on his way over there." He smiles as if he's just delivered the best news.

It is, but I'm going to miss this. Being in the same space as him and knowing I'm wanted here.

"Do I need to take off work?" I nibble on my bottom

lip. Taking off my first week on the job probably isn't a great decision, but this is a good reason. It's not like I'm blowing off work.

"Nope. That's why I'm going in late. I'm one of the bosses and as long as I get what I need to done before the weekend rush, everything will be gravy." He kisses my cheek before taking a step back. "And I already sent Eric a text. He can bring Lexi home today if I can't leave the winery."

He really is too good to me. Conrad would never have taken the initiative. One of these days I'll stop comparing the two. But it's still early for us. Not even a week. I may be open to us seeing where this goes, but I still need to protect my heart…and Lexi's.

"I was going to have Parker pick her up, but she hasn't even met him yet. Hopefully that'll change soon."

"You're telling your family?"

"Absolutely. You already know my siblings love you. They have since we were kids. And they're going to adore Lexi. Especially Piper. They've invited us to game night if you're up for it."

"Sure. I don't think Lexi has any plans. At least, not that she's told me about."

He gives me another hug before backing out of the room. "I'll let you get ready. If I stay in here there's a chance, you'll be late for work."

I roll my eyes and toss a pillow at him. "You're ridiculous." Not going to lie, I love it. He shows me he wants me, and I know it's not because he gets something out of it.

A quick glance at the clock tells me I need to get my butt in gear. I finish applying my makeup and settle for a braid over my shoulder. It's the one day a week we can dress casually and I'm taking advantage of it.

I grab my purse from the dresser and dig around for my keys, pulling the one to my house off it. Making copies of it is next on my list of things to do. Lexi needs one, and at least Miles. Though, if I'm being honest, I'll probably have one made for Peter as well. He's the closest should anything happen.

"Lexi, are you ready?" I call down the hall as I leave the room.

"Almost. Give me two minutes." She's already pushing the time crunch. She gets to school early now because of my job. But soon she'll be able to drive herself. Well, as soon as I get the course information.

"Here you go." I hold the key out for Peter. "Crap, I don't have time to take Alice out."

"Don't worry about it, I've got her."

"Thank you." He sweeps me into his arms and kisses me.

"Get a room," Lexi says as she moves to the kitchen.

"She woke up on the wrong side of the bed this morning," Peter whispers in my ear before letting me go.

"That's how it is with her. I never know how the day's going to be until our first interaction." I glance in the direction she went. "I guess she stayed up too late reading."

"Hopefully it was a good book." He pats my ass as I walk away from him. "Get going before you're late to work. I'll let you know what the plumber says."

CALLIE

Any updates?

We've been slammed with calls today. I've got appointments booked for the firm for the next month. People will be lucky if we can get them in before the tax deadline at this rate. This is the first chance I've had to look at my phone all day, and I don't see anything from Peter. Maybe there were more issues and he didn't want to tell me until I get home.

PETER

Everything is fixed. You can go to my house or yours after work. Just let me know. We have game night at Piper's tonight. I just need to know where to scoop you up from.

CALLIE

That was fast. Tell the plumber to call me so I can pay him. And we'll go to your house, it's easier since you're on the same property.

PETER

It's taken care of. I'll see you at home.

CALLIE

You didn't have to do that.

I swear he's going to be the death of me. He can't just swoop in and take care of all my problems. We'll have to talk about this sooner or later. I've been living on my own for well over a year.

I'm almost scared to ask him why. The phone on my desk rings and stops me from texting him back. He's lucky.

"Hernandez Accounting Firm, how can I help you?"

The person on the other end of the line is panicking that we won't have any appointments for her, and I do my best to assuage her fears. Within a few minutes we have an appointment booked and I just know the rest of my day is going to be more of the same. The only bright spot is the note I find inside my lunchbox.

You're hot. Let's make out.

He's so unserious. I'm happy I bring out this side of him, though.

Peter isn't at the house when I get there. But I remember him saying Friday nights begin their busy time. Lexi is in her room listening to music. I hope my brother knows he now has competition over that space. She's already added a few of her decorations to the wall and staked her claim.

I knock on the door so I don't scare her. She hates it when she doesn't hear or see me. "How was school?"

She takes off her headphones and sets them on the bed

beside her. "It was good. I'm finally fitting into my place and making friends."

"That's good." I pat her hand. "Are you up for game night at Peter's sister's house tonight?"

"What kind of games?"

"Honestly, there's no telling with this family. But expect it to be competitive."

Lexi rubs her hands together with a grin. "Then I'm totally in."

"Oh, before I forget. We can go home tomorrow. The plumber fixed all the problems today."

I expect her to be happy. She'll be back in her own space. But her face falls. "Cool. We'll still come over here a lot, right?"

"I'm sure we will. It'd be kind of hard to date someone without going to their house."

"Good. I like it here. I like our house, too. But the aesthetic Peter has is immaculate." Her eyes wander over the room with all its rustic vibes. "And I don't want Miles to make this room gross again."

"Well, you can let him know he has to clean up after himself."

"Good." She stands and moves to the dresser in the corner of the room. "I'll get ready for game night."

As I'm closing her door, Peter comes through the hallway. "Sorry I'm late. We got a huge shipment of bottles. I had to find a place to store them."

"It's okay. I just got home." I point to the door behind me. "Lexi's getting ready to head to Piper's."

He gives me a quick kiss before heading to the bedroom. "I'm going to change really quick."

"I should probably do the same. I don't want to go in

jeans." Spending a second longer in work attire is too much.

"Need some help getting into your leggings?" Peter winks at me. "Or out of them?"

"We'll never make it if you help me. Besides, Lexi is literally right there." I point at her door.

"Fine," he grumbles. He's adorable when he pouts.

I grab my leggings and a sweatshirt from the room and head to the bathroom. I know if I'm in there with him, all bets are off. We don't want to scar my poor child for life.

"Is everyone ready?" Peter calls out as I'm opening the bathroom door.

"Yep." Lexi comes out of her room with headphones in one hand and a book in the other.

"The point of game night is to play games and enjoy each other's company, right?" Peter glances from her to me.

"If I can't take my book, I'm not going." Lexi sticks out her tongue, knowing full well the argument won't stick.

"Fine. Take your book." He motions for her to walk down the hallway first. "But humor my siblings, please. I don't know that they could take being scorned by a teenager."

"I make no promises." She grins and heads down the hallway.

I follow her, and I can feel Peter's eyes on my butt as he walks behind me. The soft whistle might be another sign.

We're pulling up to Piper's house a couple of minutes later. I guess that's a perk of living on the same property. You can have someone at your house in minutes if things go awry.

"We're here." Peter calls out as he opens the door.

"We're in the living room. Foods in the kitchen," Piper yells back.

"This is going to be a loud night, isn't it?" Lexi whispers beside me.

"Most likely."

We trail behind Peter to the living room. All the Summers kids are here except for Pierce. Thinking about it now, maybe that's why he's so grumpy. He never gets invited to the fun activities. I'll bring it up to Peter later. It has to be isolating.

Everybody looks the same, just older. Time hasn't changed any of them. They don't realize how lucky they are for that.

"Y'all remember Callie." Everyone waves and Piper comes in for a hug. "And this is Alexandra, her daughter. Lexi, this is Piper, her boyfriend Beau, Paula, Parker, and Phillip."

"Hey," she gives a quick wave before Piper sweeps her up into a hug.

"It's so nice to properly meet you. How are you liking Asheville? I'm sure it's different form your last school."

"Asheville is smaller, but I've made a few friends."

"That's great." Piper claps and moves to the table. "Okay, so we have a couple of different games we can play tonight. But I have like five card decks so I think we should play cards."

"I'm cool with whatever." Lexi announces, already making herself a part of the group. I wish I had that confidence when I was her age. She's her own person and commands a room like nobody I've ever seen. It's no wonder she's already making friends.

"Cards it is." Piper scoops up the decks of cards to cut and shuffle them. "Alexandra has spoken."

"You can call me Lexi." She grins. Just like that they've earned a special place in my daughter's heart.

This has always been something I've loved about this family. They take you in as one of their own, no questions asked. We're now part of the fold.

twenty-five

· · ·

peter

THERE'S nothing quite like your family accepting the person you're dating. The only exception being Pierce. I haven't even told him I'm dating anyone. Though, I'm sure he's heard it through the grapevine by now. As much as I love my family, secrets aren't their strong suit. Now I only need my parents to come back from their travels. They're going to love Lexi I just know it.

My phone dings with a text.

CALLIE

Let me know when you're on your way.
Your brother keeps bugging about when
you'll be here.

The past couple of weeks we've been rotating houses for game nights and just hanging out. This week it's at Callie's house. I tried to offer my house, but Paula said it's not big enough. Which is something I need to think about for the future.

I would have been able to leave with the rest of my siblings if Pierce hadn't derailed my day. Now they're having fun without me.

PETER

Which brother?

CALLIE

Parker

Of course it's him. He's all about instant gratification and thinks the world revolves around him. Not that I blame him. He has charisma and people flock to him. It's actually kind of annoying. But it's who he is.

PETER

Figures. I'll be there as soon as I can.
Pierce gave me a bunch of shit to do late
in the day.

CALLIE

Of course he did. Oh, I also invited Eric
and his crew. Lexi asked if we could so
she's not the only kid.

PETER

That's cool. I'm hurrying as much as I can.

I would have been done by now if Pierce had given me the list of bottles that needed to be poured this morning. But, no, he waited until we were busy and knew I'd be rushing bottles to the main house.

I don't understand why he can't just let me be.

Working all the time isn't something I want to do anymore. Especially when a lot of it was unpaid labor. Which is wild considering I'm one of the owners. But Pierce has decided he's the main boss and needs to learn how to delegate better. Piper and Parker are upfront with the customers because they possess the charm our customers love. Phillip can do some of what I do.

Pulling out my phone, I open up our company shared document and add a note for the upcoming meeting. He'll probably complain about it, but I don't care. I had plans, and him handing me work that didn't need to be done today, put a damper on them.

I glance at the progress I've made. Only ten more to go.

"Why are you in such a rush?" Pierce's voice echoes through the room, and I almost knock a bottle over.

"Because I have a date." He doesn't need to know about the game nights, even if tonight is more of a dinner. Not right now when I'm pissed at him.

"With who?" As if he doesn't know.

"Callie." I keep working. There's no way in hell I'm going to let him pull me away from what I'm doing.

"Miles's little sister?" He laughs. "Isn't she a little, young for you?"

"She's two years younger, Pierce. Why do you care?"

"I don't." He preps the next bottle. "I saw your note on the meeting agenda."

"Is it a problem?"

"Not really. It'll be up to you to make sure Phillip's handling things okay. And if he screws up...that's on you."

"You realize he knows how to do all of this, right?" I

glare at him and wave my hand around the building. "He grew up in this business the same way we did."

"He doesn't have any motivation. He takes too long to do one thing."

I don't tell him it's because he's bored out of his mind. If he goes any faster, he won't have anything to do. The last thing he wants is to be caught sitting around and get yelled at.

"Phillip will do what he needs to."

"You can get out of here. I'll finish up."

"Really?"

He must be tired of getting the cold shoulder. He likes to dish it out, but has never liked being on the receiving end. Maybe if he wasn't such a jerk people would like him more. I still can't believe it's taken me this long to realize how awful he can be.

"Yeah. Go on your date."

I'm not arguing with him. "See you tomorrow morning." Without waiting for a response, I hightail it to my truck. I'm not even going to stop at my house to change. The last thing I need is for Callie to think I'm the same as Conrad. I'd much rather be with her than bottling wine.

In less than five minutes I'm pulling into Callie's driveway. All of my siblings are here and I see Eric's car parked at the very end of the line.

A quick glance in the rearview mirror to make sure I'm presentable and I'm out of my truck. Before I have a chance to knock on the door, Callie is opening it up.

"Finally." The relief on her face breaks me. That asshole made her second guess everything. Always on the search for a possible lie.

"Yes, finally." I pull her into my arms and my lips crash

into hers. She won't have any doubt about how I feel toward her. Once I'm sure she's gotten the message, I break the kiss. "The party can get started," I call out.

"Callie, you can never leave this family again." Paula grabs a glass and pours herself some wine. "I don't know what you've done to my brother, but this is the happiest I think I've ever seen him."

"Well, I did just buy a house. I think I'm going to be around for a while." She beams at my older sister. I'm not sure Paula knows how much she's reassured Callie with that statement. But I'm glad she knows how happy she's made me.

"Good. I don't think I can take another day of Peter moping around and simply existing." Parker adds.

"I don't mope." What is this gang up on Peter night?

"Sure, you don't." Parker rolls his eyes. "Can we eat now? I'm starving."

"Dig in." Callie gives the go ahead and takes my hand in hers. She really is a dream come true for me.

Parker is the last person to leave, and I'm practically shoving him out the door. I love my brother, I really do, but I need him to go. Now that Callie is back in her own house, we don't get as much time together.

"I think we just hosted our first successful event." Callie collapses on the couch and I pick up her legs to sit under them. "That was exhausting. It's been forever since I've had people over."

"You're a natural." I grab her fuzzy sock covered foot and dig my thumbs into the arch.

"Oh my God, that feels good." She moans, and damn she needs to stop doing things like that. We made an agreement no sex while Lexi is in the house. Callie feels weird about it, and I'm going to respect those wishes.

"You deserve it. Do you want to go lie down? Me and Lexi can clean up."

"I think Piper and Beau took care of most of it. There may be a few dishes left. They can wait, though." She covers her face with her arm and for a second, I think she's fallen asleep. "Is it just me or is it odd us not being in the same space all the time?"

It's like she plucked the thought out of my head.

"Not just you. The house feels empty when I go home." I lean my head against the back of the couch. "I know we weren't sleeping in the same bed, but you were right down the hall."

"Agreed. I don't think I like it."

Me either, but we need to make sure we're going at a steady pace. Even with Lexi doing her best to get us together, I don't want us to go too fast. At least not yet, it's only been a couple of weeks. But...I already know I want forever with her. In a lot of ways it's like we picked up in our friendship where we left off.

"I can stay here tonight and leave early for work."

"I don't want you to cut into sleep." She feels around the couch. "And my sofa won't fit you at all."

"It'll be fine." It's literally the same size as the one at my house. "I can stack all the pillows to the side."

"Okay."

Well, that was easy. I figured she'd put up more of a fight. She rolls over to her side and pulls her knees up. She'll be passing out in about five minutes.

As soon as I know she's asleep, I slide out from under her legs and head to the kitchen. Lexi is putting up food and getting everything in order.

"Need some help?" I roll up the sleeves of my shirt before heading straight the sink and pile of dishes. There isn't a lot, it's big stuff that takes up more room.

"You don't have to do those by hand. We have a dishwasher." She points at the appliance in question.

"I'm good. There's something relaxing about washing dishes. Besides you shouldn't be doing this by yourself. It was my family that crashed your house." I fill up the sink with water and soap.

"They're really nice. They did a lot, including taking out the trash. I hate doing it when it's cold."

Lexi liking my family is important to me. I want her to feel comfortable with them since we do a lot together.

"I'm glad you get along with them. It's not always easy when we're all together. There's a lot of us." I finish washing the last item before rinsing it off and setting it in the drain on the counter. That didn't take long at all. I turn toward Lexi to see how she's doing with clean up.

She stacks a container on top of a stack of them on the table. Hopefully they have room in the fridge. "Yeah, but y'all are funny."

That's a term nobody has used to describe me. Parker was right earlier when he said I was only existing. I never had anything in my life I wanted to do more for... until now.

"Are you going to the Valentine's event with me and your mom?" I want to make sure there's space for her at our table.

"Gross, no. I don't want to hang out with a bunch of

adults making googly eyes at each other on Valentine's Day." A shiver runs through her, and I can't stop from chuckling.

"What are you going to do?"

"Abby is having a girl's only sleepover. We're going to watch cheesy romcoms and play games."

"That sounds like a fun night."

"Yep. I need to buy some cute pajamas and gifts for the girls."

She's open with me and I like that I can be that for her. I'm guessing her father isn't. But I don't want to ask.

"Do you know what your mom is wearing to the dinner next week?" I need to make sure I match, and I want to get her flowers to complement her outfit.

"Nope. I don't think she's picked out anything. I want to get my stuff tomorrow so maybe we can shop for something for her."

I like the way her mind works. Reaching into my back pocket, I pull out my wallet and grab one of my cards. "Here, use this for your shopping trip." Her eyes light and her hand shoots out. "Don't go wild, but you can get whatever you need for the sleepover and your mom something to wear. Make sure it's something she loves, and not something she settles for."

"Okay." She waits for me to put my card in her hand. "You know, I think I like you and Mom dating."

"Whys that?"

"Because you make her happy." She stares at the card in her hand. "And you take care of her instead of the other way around. I try, but she has this whole thing about it because she's the parent. It's nice seeing her carry less stress."

"I'll keep doing it as long as she lets me." I had a great example growing up. Dad still dotes on Mom and they've been together over forty years. I want that with Callie.

"Good. Are you going home?" She gestures toward the containers on the table while sliding the card into her pocket. "We have a ton of food. You can take some with you."

"Nope. I'm going to crash on the couch."

"Oh." She grabs the containers and I rush to open the refrigerator door. "You don't have to sleep on the couch, you know."

"Whys that?"

She slides the containers onto various shelves before turning to me. "You are both grown-ups. It's weird you aren't sleeping in the same bed."

"Okay." I take a step back.

She points her finger at me. "But no funny business. These walls are thin."

Now I've been properly warned by a teenager. I never thought that would happen in my entire life. I wait until she leaves the kitchen, turn off all the lights, and head to the living room.

Callie is fast asleep. I scoop her into my arms and carry her to her bedroom. She usually does a routine at night to get ready for bed, but I don't think she will tonight.

Her eyes open a bit, and she glances around. "What are you doing?"

"Putting you in bed."

She wiggles her legs for me to put her down. I pull back the blankets and wait until she's comfortable to place the covers over her. I take off my pants and shirt before climbing into the other side of the bed.

"I thought we agreed not to sleep in the bed together."

"Lexi gave me permission. But no shenanigans." I move next to her until her back against my chest, and I wrap an arm around her waist to close any gaps.

A contented sigh escapes her lips. "Oh, okay."

She snuggles into me and damn this feels like home.

twenty-six

. . .

callie

PETER IS GONE when I wake up. I vaguely remember his lips on my cheek, but I thought I was dreaming.

Everything about last night was perfect. The food and company. I was bummed Peter was late.

Each insecurity I had when I was with Conrad crept its way into my gut. It took everything in me to push them away. Peter isn't anything like Conrad. He's kind, giving, and bends over backward for those he cares about. He's always been that way.

"You're finally up." Lexi says as she walks into my room. "You should probably get ready."

She's dressed in a sweater and jeans. A touch of mascara darkening her lashes. "Where are we going? I didn't think we had any plans today."

"We didn't…until I remembered I need things for my sleepover with Abby." She runs her fingers through a strand of hair and mutters something under her breath.

"What was that?" She only talks like that when she's not ready for me to hear whatever she wants me to buy. We go through this all the time, you'd think she'd stop.

"I said and to find you a dress for Friday night." She turns and exits the room to avoid an argument.

There are a ton of dresses in my closet. I don't need a new one. I throw the blankets off me and hurry over to make sure I'm not lying to Lexi...or myself. The hangers scrape against the rod and I'm beginning to think I should have had coffee before going on this endeavor.

That one is frumpy. Too bright. None of the dresses can pass for a date night dress. A black one catches my eye and I pull it off the hanger. I haven't worn this one in years. I wonder if it still fits.

I change from my pajamas into the dress. It's a little snug, but it'll pass. My steps are slow as I walk into Lexi's room.

"Absolutely not."

"Why? It's an appropriate length and goes with heels I already have."

"Mom." She covers her face with one hand and shakes her head. "You look like you're going to a funeral. Is that the message you want to send Peter on Valentine's of all days?"

I move to her full-length mirror on her closet door. "It's not that bad."

"It's not that good, either." She mutters loud enough for me to hear. "Look, I was told to make sure you buy a dress you love today. I'm not going to break that agreement."

She was told? "Who did you make this agreement with?"

"Peter." She shrugs and reaches into her bag, pulling out a card. "He said to get what I need for the sleepover and buy you a dress. Don't freak out, he told me not to go wild."

I reach for the card in her hand and she yanks it back.

"We can't let him pay for our things. I have a job."

"Mom, he knows that. He's trying to help."

Clearly, I'm not going to win this argument with my teenage daughter. I turn on my heel and march back to my room. My phone is on my nightstand and when I reach for it, there's a message from Peter.

PETER

Good morning gorgeous. I didn't want to
wake you. Have fun today.

Instead of texting him back, I hit the button to call him. It rings four times before he answers.

"We cannot use your card to go shopping. What were you thinking giving a fifteen-year-old your credit card?"

There's a noise coming from the other end of the line. At first, I think it's wind or something, but then I realize. He's...laughing.

"Lexi is responsible. I have zero worries giving her my card. I would have given it to you, if I thought you would actually take it."

"Because you know—"

He cuts me off. "I want to do this for you. I know you have a job and all that jazz, but let me do this for you. Consider it a Valentine's gift for both you and Lexi."

"It's too much, Peter. You've already done so much for us."

"Because I wanted to. Please, let me have this. If it'll make you feel any better, you can pay for the wine."

"Um, no. You get that with the tickets for the event."

"How do you know?"

"I was talking to Parker about it last night. But he also said you and your date are free because y'all own the place. So, nice try."

"Fine, we'll think of something else. You can take me out to eat one night."

This man infuriates me sometimes, even if I appreciate what he's trying to do. Everything he's done for us has been out of kindness. He expects nothing in return. There's no use arguing with him because he's not going to back down.

"Fine."

"Thank you." I can hear the smile in his voice. Dammit, why am I smiling? "You and Lexi have a fun girl's day. I'll come by after we get off work."

"Okay." I love you is on the tip of my tongue, but it's too soon for that. I can't forget we're just now getting together even if we've known each other our whole lives and I've loved him just as long. "See you later."

"Bye." He hangs up as soon as the words leave his mouth.

We had to go to the next town over. As much as I love Asheville, they don't have much in the way of clothing stores. Well, except for the boutique ones. And I'm not that type of girl.

"Mom, come look at this dress." Lexi calls from a couple of sections down. She could have come and got me. Not yell at me from across the store. I'm pretty sure I did the same thing at her age, though.

I hurry over to where she's standing so she doesn't disturb the other shoppers. She's holding up a bright red dress. It's strapless and looks way too short for me to wear. It looks more like something she would wear to a formal dance.

Except it is beautiful. If I were about seventeen years younger, I'd snatch it up in a heartbeat.

"Absolutely not." Lexi shoves the dress at me. "My butt would hang out."

She rolls her eyes. "It's a form-fitting dress, Mom. It's going to fit you like a glove." Grabbing my arm, she leads me toward the dressing room. "Please, try it on."

She's pleading with me. I'll try it on to humor her. Maybe then she'll see I'm much too old for this dress. "Fine."

"Is this what it feels like when you force me to try on clothes during school shopping?"

"Probably."

"Yikes. Remind me to remember this moment."

I roll my eyes and go into an empty room and begin stripping off my t-shirt and leggings. Now I need to put the dress on. It looks like I need to slide it up my body isn't of the over. I can't reach the zipper, though.

Cracking open the door, I whisper for Lexi. "Can you help me?"

I turn around so she can't see the full look. She tries to get on her tiptoes to see the mirror, but I block her.

"This is so unfair." She mutters as she pulls up the zipper.

I smooth out the dress and take a step to the side to let her in the room with me. "What do you think?"

Lexi's eyes widen and she claps her hands. "I think I told you so. Mom, you look hot!"

I don't know about that part. But…I love it. It hugs my curves in all the right places. The dress is shorter than I would normally wear, way shorter. My butt doesn't hang out, though. Even my legs look longer.

"Do you think Peter will like it?" Is it weird that I'm asking my teenager this? Under normal circumstances, I'd probably say yes. However, she's been orchestrating this since she saw the way we interacted that first night we saw each other.

"If he doesn't, he's dead to me." She twirls her finger for me to spin around. "Actually, you might make him pass out."

She's ridiculous. "Let's hope he doesn't."

"Now, we need to find you the perfect shoes and accessories."

"Didn't Peter tell you not to go wild?" I give her a stern look.

"Mom, that dress is discounted. I know how to shop, I learned from the best." She grins at me. "Get changed so we can finish the look."

"Yes, ma'am." I laugh and turn my back to her. "Can you undo the zipper now?" She does what I ask and heads back in the hallway. "I'll be out in a few."

I change and put the dress back on the hanger. Never in a million years did I think I would look good in a dress like this. Even when I was Lexi's age, I never would've had the confidence. That all changes today.

I open the door and Lexi is still grinning from ear to ear. "Let's get the rest of the outfit. Oh, and I think I know what kind of pajamas I want to get for the sleepover."

"What about the gifts?"

"I'm thinking mini spa kits we can do while we're there. You know face masks and stuff like that."

"Good idea." I fold the dress over my arm and we make our way to the shoe department. "Peter is coming over after he gets off work. I'm thinking pizza for dinner."

"I could eat pizza." She sees the aisle of heels and she's off. It's going to be a long afternoon.

"Did you find a dress?" Peter asks as he brings his plate to the table.

"Yep." I refuse to give him any hints about it.

"You'll love it," Lexi adds before taking a bite of her food. "And I'm all set for my sleepover. I'll give you your card after dinner. It's in my room."

"Sounds good." His foot touches my foot under the table. "I can't wait to show you off."

I snort and cause everyone to laugh. "We'll see."

After a few more bites, Peter clears his throat. "I have a bit of bad news, but it's not Pierce related. It's all Piper's fault this time."

"Did something happen with the event?" I'd hate for her to hit a snag in something she's excited about. She was telling me all about it during dinner last night.

"No, we have the caterers set and all that. Whoopsie Daisy is going to come out and do the floral arrangements for the tables. But…Piper needs to hang a million lights in the trees, which is going to take me a while. So, I'll be working late."

"Oh." I can't help the way my voice falls. He's nothing like Conrad. It's the line I have to repeat in my head.

"But, I can come here when I leave. Or, y'all can come to my place." He takes another bite of his pizza and his eyes widen as if a lightbulb went off in his head. "Even better, you can come to the winery. I'll be working, but I'm sure Piper would love some help with her vision. She's refusing any input from us guys, even Parker."

That actually sounds kind of fun, and I love hanging out with his sisters. "What do you think Lexi?"

"I'm totally in. I can even bring a book to read if I get bored."

"Or, your homework." I glance at her.

"Yeah, yeah." She waves me off. "If I have homework, I'll bring it. Just suck all the fun out of it."

"Homework should come first." Peter adds.

"As if you ever stayed on top of it." I shake my head at him. "How many times did you turn in late assignments and have to do extra credit so you wouldn't upset your mom?"

"Which is why I said it comes first." He sticks his tongue out at me.

"Are you staying the night again?" Lexi asks before taking her plate to the sink.

"I'm not sure."

"Please. I want to show you the stuff I got to take to Abby's. And maybe watch a movie."

Peter glances over at me to see if it's okay. He may take

care of me in every other way, but he lets me know this choice will always remain with me.

"I'm fine with it. But I get to pick the movie."

These are the nights I'm beginning to love. Nothing extravagant, just a quiet evening with two of my favorite people.

twenty-seven

. . .

peter

THIS WEEK FEELS like the work has been so much harder than normal. We don't do events like this often. At least, not yet. We did a big holiday party for Christmas and folks brought their families. This one is for adults only, though. Piper wants it perfect so we can gauge if these types of things are worth the effort.

Callie and Lexi came out when they could. But we were serious when we said homework comes first. Maybe if I'd taken it more seriously like some of my siblings, I would have options outside of the winery. Not that I don't love working here. This was a place built by family, and I take a lot of pride in it.

"It's a good thing we closed the winery today." Piper stands next to me and admires everything we've done. "There's no way we would have finished in time to get ready."

"Yeah, that was a good call even if Pierce was mad about it."

She waves the comment away. "He'll get over it. The ticket sales we had for the event more than covers what we make on a typical Friday. We're not losing any profits. Even with the cost of catering."

"At least Paula, and Whoopsie Daisy, are doing the arrangements at a discount."

"Yep," Piper agrees. "Perks of having a sister in an adjacent field of work."

I've never seen the winery like this. We have tables inside, of course, but the whole yard is decked out with tables and heat lamps. The perfect place for folks who want some privacy or need to get some air.

"Should we head out and get ready?" I'm anxious to see the dress Callie bought. Lexi told me it was red, but that's it. Plus, I still need to run by Whoopsie Daisy and pick up the flowers I ordered.

"Absolutely." Piper gives me a half hug. "Thank you for all the help this week. From you, Callie, and Lexie. You have no idea how much I appreciate it."

"Don't even worry about it." I give her a tight squeeze before letting go. "We need to be here at six, right?"

"Yep. Now get out of here." I don't need to be told again.

Bouquet in hand, my steps are slow as I approach Callie's front door. Why are my hands sweaty? It's like we're going on a first date, or a dance. I haven't been this nervous since I was much, much younger.

I raise a hand and knock on the door. It takes a few minutes for it to open. I expected to see Callie, but Lexi is grinning at me.

"She's almost ready." She gestures for me to come in, and I follow her into the living room after closing the door. "You look a lot different dressed up."

"Thanks?" Does she mean I look horrible when I come over in my work clothes?

"It's a compliment," she whispers and turns toward the hallway. "I'm gonna check on Mom. I'll be right back."

I hear a door close and take that as my sign to sit down. Anything is better than pacing around the room. Though now I don't know what to do. The TV isn't on, and Alice is snoring in her bed on the other side of the room. It's way too quiet.

After what feels like an eternity, the door opens and Lexi comes rushing into the living room. "She's coming out now."

I stand and turn toward the hallway. The anticipation builds as footsteps approach us. With the way Lexi is acting, I'm not sure what to expect.

The flowers fall from my hand the second Callie steps into the room. She is stunning. Her long brown hair falls in loose curls over her shoulder. The dress is bold and clings to her body in all the right places. Her legs seem to go on for miles and she's taller with the silver heels on her feet. What the hell did I do to deserve this woman?

"You're gorgeous." The words slip out of my mouth, barely above a whisper.

Callie's cheeks redden. "Thank you."

I bend down and grab the flowers, inspecting them for damage. "These are for you."

She studies the red roses as she takes them from my hand. "They're beautiful."

"I told you he'd like it. And he didn't pass out." Lexi breaks the moment and both of us laugh.

"Do we need to take you to Abby's?" I ask.

"Nope. Her mom is picking me up in a bit. I wanted to be here for the grand reveal."

I take a step closer to Callie. "Shall we, then?"

She hands the flowers to her daughter. "Can you put these in water for me? Have fun tonight. If you need anything, I have my phone. I'm sure Peter has his, too."

I pat my pocket to show her that I do have my phone. Piper said I had to have it on me at all times for the day.

"Yep. You kids have fun." She pushes her mom close to me. "But not too much fun." She winks and darts off to the kitchen.

Callie loops her arm through mine and we're off for the night. I'm still trying to figure out how I'm going to handle her in this dress without carrying her back to my place.

The lights on the trees were a good idea. It looks like a fairy wonderland. Piper has good instincts when it comes to things like this.

I park the truck at my parent's house because people won't be over here, and I don't want to take up space where a valet will be parking cars for the guests. The last thing I expect to see is my parent's car off to the side.

"Mom and Dad are home," I say in awe.

Callie looks over at me. "Wouldn't they normally be?"

"Not lately. Since they retired, they've been traveling

around the country and taking cruises." I shake my head, but I'm happy for them. They deserve it after all the years they've put in here. I hope I can do the same one day… with Callie by my side.

"That sounds exciting."

"Yeah, they send us pictures all the time." I glance from her to the house. "Do you want to re-meet them?"

She glances at what she's wearing. "Aren't I a bit over-dressed?"

"Nope."

Shrugging, she turns to me with a smile. "Sure."

I turn off the truck, hop out and rush around to the passenger side to help Callie out. It's a bit difficult for her with the heels and everything. I pretty much have to pick her up and set her on the ground. I pull off my jacket and set it around her arms. I asked if she needed a jacket before we left her house, but she said it would ruin the look.

She slides her hands into mine as we step on the porch. I see Dad's silhouette in the window and don't bother knocking.

"Is this something you and your siblings do? Just walk into each other's houses?"

"Pretty much. There's pretty much zero privacy in this family."

"It's cool y'all are so open with each other."

"It's a blessing and a curse." I laugh. "Mom? Dad?"

"You're the first one who's noticed we're home." Mom rushes up to me and gives me a hug. "Who's this?" Dad comes up behind her and gives me a nod. He's not big on hugging.

"Y'all remember Callie? Miles's sister?" I give her and

a quick squeeze. "She moved back to Asheville and we're dating."

"It's about time." Mom claps her hands together before pulling Callie away from me and into a hug. "I saw the way both of you looked at each other as kids and always wondered why nothing ever came from it."

"I didn't get my head out of my a— butt." I change the word at the last second when Dad gives me a look.

"Well, I'm happy for you." She glances at the clock on the wall. "Don't you need to get up to the winery. You know your sister is probably freaking out."

"Yeah, I only wanted to re-introduce y'all so you weren't taken by surprise. You know since you're actually home."

"We'll be home for a while this time." Dad says at my accusation. "We'll see you over there."

They are shooing us out the door. I wrap my arm around Callie to keep her as warm as I can on the walk over. Luckily, it isn't a long walk. Their house is the closest to the actual business.

"Wow." Callie gasps as we come into the main yard. "This is gorgeous. I want to take a picture of it before we leave. I'm sure Lexi would love something like that for her birthday."

I pull my phone out of my pocket and step away from her. The lights are glowing behind her as I snap a photo. "There. Now you have one."

"Thank you." She pulls my jacket tighter over her shoulders.

My brothers and sisters are waiting for us in the building most of the event will take place. The catering staff is done setting up, and the Whoopsie Daisy crew are finishing the tables.

"It looks fantastic, Piper." I tell my sister. "Your vision truly came to life."

"Thank you." She clasps her hands to her chest. "I couldn't have done it without y'all."

"Most of us." Pierce mutters under his breath.

"What does that mean?" I ask.

"You haven't been here as much as you used to because you're too busy playing house with a girl you used to know." He crosses his arms as if somehow that makes his statement more important.

Callie gasps and that's what does me in. I feel her try to pull away from me, but I'm not letting that happen. She has enough insecurities after everything her ex-husband pulled. She needs to know she doesn't have anything to worry about with me.

"That woman is standing right here. You're only mad because I'm done being your fucking lap dog and no longer spending all my time up here. Callie is the woman I love, and it shouldn't be a problem for me to be home and spend time with her. Just because this," I wave my hands to encompass the winery, "is your life, doesn't mean it has to be the rest of ours. I'm so sick of you playing at being our overlord. It's not what Dad did, and it's not what he wants for us. He's always valued family over work. Your refusal to do that is what is going to make us hate the business our family has built."

The rest of our siblings are staring at me as if I've lost my mind. In my entire life, I've never spoken to Pierce like this. I point one finger at him because I'm done tiptoeing around the fact he's tearing this family, and business, apart. "You need to change and figure out what's important."

He doesn't say anything. Only stomps out of the building and we're left to deal with the aftermath of my outburst.

"Holy shit." Parker says. "That was epic."

I half expect them to slow clap like they do in the movies, but Piper must know I need some time with Callie. "Okay, everyone. Let's make sure the lastminute things are done. People will arrive soon."

Once the family is out of earshot, I turn to Callie. "I'm sorry about that. Someone needed to say it, and I guess it's only right it was me."

She places a hand against my chest. "You love me?"

That's what she got out the whole thing? I guess I did say it in the most unromantic way possible.

"Yes, Callie, I love you." I place my hand over hers. "I'm pretty sure I've been half in love with you my entire life. I didn't know what to do with the feelings back then. But, now I do."

I bend down and place a soft kiss to her lips. As much as I want to ravage her, this isn't the time or place. Even if I'm not technically working, I'm still required to be here tonight.

She melts into me and pulls away when she hears a throat clear behind us.

"Not to kill the vibe, but people are pulling in." Parker taps my shoulder. "So be all romantic when you get home. I know I will be."

"With who?" I glance over at him. "This whole evening is about couples and you don't have a date."

"That's where you're wrong. Piper included singles

tickets and we have our own little area. I'll be leaving here with one."

"You're way too cocky for your own good."

He shrugs and walks away. I turn my attention back to Callie. "We'll stay until after dinner then we're out of here."

"We can stay as long as we need to." She pats my cheek. "And I love you, too."

After all these years, we're finally able to say the words we always wanted to. There's no way I'm ever letting her go a day in her life without showing her how much her and Lexi mean to me. Even if it's only been a short time, I can't imagine my lift without them in it.

epilogue

. . .

one year later

"MOM." Lexi barges into my room. "We're going to be late. We've been waiting on you for like thirty minutes."

"You have a license now. You and Abby can head up there." I'm putting on the final touches of my makeup. It's going to be hard to top last year's look for the annual Valentine's dinner at Starlit Fields, but I think I accomplished it. "I can drive up there myself. It's not like it's far."

"I know, but Peter and Piper said we have to get there at a specific time. There's no point in all of us taking our vehicles when we're coming back to the same place."

She's not wrong. Peter's staying here for a while. He's doing renovations on his house to add on some rooms and bathrooms before we move in with him. We toyed with idea of him moving in here, but Lexi said she'd rather have her room at Peter's.

"Okay. Can you get my shrug? I'm not making the same mistake this year."

"Yep. I'll even get the car started as long as you're almost done."

"Give me two minutes."

She runs off to start the car. They are working with the catering crew to earn extra money for the holidays. Her and Abby are also trying to save money to take a trip after they graduate in a year and a half. I'm not ready to let her go, but I think I've done a great job raising her.

I finish applying my lipstick and stand to look at the full effect. Perfect. It's not as short as the one last year but accentuates all the areas Peter loves. It is still red, though.

Lexi hands me my shrug as soon as I'm in the living room. "Can we go now?"

She's acting off tonight. Maybe it's nerves because she's working, but I feel like it's something more. She'll tell me when she's ready.

It doesn't take us long to get to Peter's parent's house. They aren't here. They decided to do a couples cruise after being home for a while. I don't blame them. They are doing things they enjoy together, and I can't wait to experience that stage of life with Peter.

Lexi turns off the car and gets out. "We have to get something from their backyard. Piper said she needs it for the dinner."

Weird. But I don't argue with her. Piper does unconventional things when it comes to marketing and events for the winery. Business continues to grow, and they're hiring more people all the time.

I follow my daughter and her best friend to the backyard, unsure if they need help with what we're getting.

My heels clack along the pathway in the stillness of the night and I come to a stop as soon as we're through the gate.

Peter is standing next to the picnic table we also used to gather around for snacks in the summer. There are lights strung across the backyard and the girls are nowhere in sight.

"Where did the girls go? They said they needed something for the event."

"They're around." He rushes over to me and his eyes trail my entire body. "You look stunning. I need to pick up my game if I'm going to look good on your arm."

I roll my eyes and look around the yard. "What do we need to get? Your sister will blow a gasket if we're not there soon."

"Come with me." He takes my hand in his and I follow him to the table we sat at when we were kids.

In the dim light I can see where each Summers kid has carved their name into the top. I run my free hand along the grooves until Peter stops on the other end. My name and Lexi's have been added to the table. The cuts look fresh and I wonder when he did it.

"We spent so much of childhood together. Many of those days ended here." He turns toward me and gets down on one knee. Oh my God. He's not…no, he can't be. "It's about time we added your names to the table since you're a part of this family now. I love you more than anything. You, and Lexi, brought me back to life. Made me see there's more to it than working and trying to prove myself. All I want to do is show you how much I love every day for the rest of my life. Will you marry me?"

I refuse to admit how much I've dreamed of hearing

that specific question from Peter. From when I was a lovesick teenager daydreaming about our future together to the day he came back into my life, no matter how hard I tried to fight it.

"Yes, Peter." He slides the ring on my finger. The perfect fit. He scoops me up as he stands and twirls me around. Clapping comes from everywhere around us. My lips meet his as he sets me down to continued cheers.

"That would have been really embarrassing if you said no." He smiles down at me.

"There isn't a lifetime where that would have happened." I glance around at the faces of all his brothers and sisters, even Pierce. Things are still rocky between them, but he's here, and that's all that matters. Piper has a phone in her hand, and I can hear their parents yelling congratulations. Miles is leaning on the fence grinning. As if he knew this would happen all along.

Lexi rushes up and throws her arms around us. "Finally. Do you have any idea how long I've been keeping this secret?"

"The two of you have got to stop plotting." I say to both of them.

Peter has the decency to look as if he's in trouble. Lexi shakes her head. "Yeah, that's not gonna happen."

"Crap." Piper yells. "Sorry, Mom and Dad. But we have to go. Have fun on your cruise." She ends the call before they have a chance to say anything. "Everyone to the main building. We have an event to put on."

Each person gives us a hug as they hurry to the golf carts waiting on the other side of the fence. I'm not sure how I didn't see them. They leave one behind.

"I'll see you later Callie." Miles wraps me in a hug.

"Are you going to the event?" It's not really his scene, and he doesn't look to be dressed for the occasion.

"Hell no." He laughs and lets me go. "I don't want to tempt fate into finding me someone to date. I'm happy as I am."

"Well, have fun with whatever you're doing."

He gives a quick wave and leaves the backyard. Both of us watch him go before Peter turns to me once again.

"I can't wait to spend the rest of my life with you." Peter kisses my forehead.

"Me too. You have no idea how happy you've made me in the last year."

"And I'll keep doing it." He glances at the golf cart. "We better get going. Piper will lose it if we're not up there soon."

"We definitely don't want to make her mad." I glance at my shoes and the grass between us the cart. "Any chance you want to carry me so my heels don't sink."

"I'll carry you anywhere." He bends down cradles me in his arms to ease the journey for me. "Is Lexi staying with Abby tonight?"

"I think so." I'm not sure where he's going with this line of questioning.

"Good. When we leave here. I want you in nothing but those heels."

Oh. "You can count on it."

Every day he shows me how much he wants me. How beautiful he thinks I am, stretch marks and all. He's broken every insecurity I had about myself and welcomed my daughter with open arms. Sometimes the wait is worth it.

acknowledgments

There's no way I would have gotten this book done without my friends and family. They gave me the space I needed to write, and cheered me on along the way.

Nessa, you are my ride or die. Thank you for coming with me to events and listening to me talk about a genre you don't even read. Here's to twenty more years of being besties!

Steph, Hallie, and Ashley, y'all make writing so much fun. And listen to me complain about my imposter syndrome. Seriously, thank you for being some of the best friends a girl could ask for.

To my Patreon members, thank you for your support. You have no idea how much it means! Steph, Lisa, and Kerli, you're the best!

To Claudia, thank you for being an amazing Alpha reader. Especially when I message you at midnight.

Aurora, thank you so much for the beautiful cover. I love it so freaking much. You've been with me since the beginning and I'm eternally grateful for all your support.

And my family…thank you for being you. Y'all make me laugh, cry, and want to scream sometimes when you interrupt my writing time. But I love you all the same. Thank you for experiencing life with me. It would be pretty boring without you.

Last, but not least, my readers. Thank you for coming along on this journey with me. Whether you've been here since Welcome to Your Life, or Blended Hearts is your first book from me, I'm so grateful for you. I hope you connect with any of my characters.

also by katrina marie

Do you want to meet more of the characters in Asheville? You can check out my books here. Or, scan the QR code to find out what some of the other residents of this small town are up to.

about the author

Katrina Marie lives in the Dallas area with her husband, two children, and fur baby. She is a lover of all things geeky and Gryffindor for life. When she's not writing you can find her at her children's sporting events, or curled up reading a book.

You can find Katrina Marie online in the following places:

Sign up for my newsletter: https://katrinamarieauthor.com/newsletter

Website: katrinamarieauthor.com

 facebook.com/katrinamarieauthor

 instagram.com/katrinamarieauthor

 bookbub.com/profile/katrina-marie

 pinterest.com/katrinamarieauthor

www.ingramcontent.com/pod-product-compliance
Lightning Source LLC
Chambersburg PA
CBHW021127190726
48288CB00008B/2541